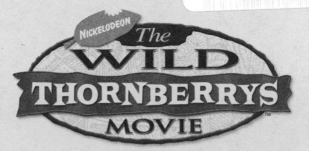

SIMON SPOTLIGHT
An imprint of Simon & Schuster Children's Publishing Division
1230 Avenue of the Americas, New York, New York 10020

Manufactured in the United States of America

First Edition
2 4 6 8 10 9 7 5 3 1

ISBN 0-689-85095-6
Library of Congress Control Number 2002104565

adapted by Cathy East Dubowski
based on the screenplay written by Kate Boutilier

Simon Spotlight/Nickelodeon

New York   London   Toronto   Sydney   Singapore

A Letter from

Eliza Thornberry

Hi! I'm Eliza Thornberry. I'm a twelve-year-old girl from an average family. I have a dad, a mom, and a teenage sister named Debbie. Well, there *is* my adopted brother, Donnie . . . we found him in the jungle. And Darwin the chimpanzee. He found us.

We live in a big safari-camper called a Commvee. It's got just about everything we need to camp anywhere. Would you believe it travels on land and water? It's the perfect house for us because we travel all over the world.

You see, my dad hosts this TV nature show, *Nigel Thornberry's Animal World,* and my mom films it.

Okay, so maybe we're not that average. And between you and me, something amazing happened to me. . . .

It's really cool, and ever since, life's never been the same. You want to know my secret? Promise not to tell anyone? Okay, the secret is . . . I can talk to animals!

Believe me, my special gift comes in handy when I'm traveling all over the world. Like the time my family traveled to Africa to study elephants. . . .

Chapter 1

Tanzania, Africa

A mother cheetah crouched on the Serengeti Plain, hiding in the tall, golden grasses. Watching. Waiting.

A herd of graceful Thomson's gazelles grazed nearby.

Suddenly the cheetah pushed off with her back legs—and sprang!

But gazelles had shared the Serengeti with cheetahs for generations and had learned to be alert. The lead male's head popped up, his curved antlers pointing skyward as he listened.

A split second later the herd took flight.

Predator and prey raced across the wide-open plain. The cheetah had the advantage: As the fastest creature on Earth, she could run up to seventy miles an hour.

The swift gazelles were not as fast. But over centuries they'd grown nimble; they had learned to dart from side to side to evade the cheetah, which ran best in a straight line.

And so they ran across the grassy plain, past a twisted acacia tree, and beyond . . . in a race that would last until one or the other grew weary of the chase. . . .

•   •   •

Just behind the acacia tree an elephant raised its thick trunk and trumpeted a call. The sound was followed by a foreign sound . . .

A giggle.

Eliza Thornberry—a twelve-year-old girl with red braids and braces—laughed as she rode high on the dusty gray back of her elephant friend Kianga.

Darwin, a gray chimpanzee in blue shorts and a striped tank top, was riding behind her, his hands tucked behind his head.

"And now," Eliza announced, "Kianga the Magnificent will walk the Circle of Destiny—"

"Oh, that sounds good," Kianga said, flapping her huge fanlike ears. As she lumbered forward Eliza hung on, but Darwin was startled and scrambled to keep from tumbling off.

"Circle of Destiny, indeed! Do you see how high off the ground we are?" he complained. "And look at those tusks! They could poke an eye out!"

"Darwin, relax," Eliza told him. "Kianga, can you take us around that tree?"

"Sure! Hey, I'll show you how our moms make us go: They nudge the back of our necks with their trunks." She reached around with her trunk and tapped Eliza on the back of her neck.

Eliza giggled, then copied the motion on the elephant's neck just above her shoulders.

"That's it," Kianga said. "And if she wanted us to turn around, she'd just nudge one side."

"Like this?" Eliza gently pressed her left foot behind Kianga's left ear.

Kianga turned sharply to the left. Darwin shrieked and grabbed on to Eliza.

"Oh, cool!" Eliza exclaimed.

"Eliza, can we go now?" Darwin said with a huff. "My butt's gone to sleep."

Eliza sighed. She could tell that Darwin wasn't having much fun. "Okay, Darwin."

Kianga slowly knelt, allowing Eliza to slide down from her back. Darwin slid right behind her and landed on the ground with a thud.

"See you later, Kianga," Eliza said.

"Bye, Eliza!" Kianga called after them as they ran toward camp. "Bye, chimp!"

Darwin dashed ahead. "Oh, I think I hear your

grandmumsy opening a fresh tin of figgy pudding!" he said to Eliza.

Eliza grinned. Darwin and his stomach! But then she froze. She heard something, and it definitely wasn't a can opener. "Shhh . . . Darwin, listen."

Darwin paused and listened too. "Uh-oh. . . ."

*   *   *

Back at the Thornberry camp, Nigel was having a cup of tea with his mother, who was visiting from England.

"It's a shame you couldn't spend more time with us, Mumsy," he said.

"Oh, two weeks is more than enough," Cordelia Thornberry replied. "You know your father gets a bit daft when left on his own too long. For all we know, he's spent the entire two weeks searching for his reading glasses."

"Good thing I take after you, eh, Mumsy?" Nigel chuckled, then called to his wife. "Uh, Marianne? Have you had any luck locating my binoculars?"

Marianne looked up from beneath the hood of the Commvee, where she was giving the engine a tune-up. "Try around your neck!" she said with a knowing smile.

Nigel glanced down in surprise, and guffawed to find his binoculars right there.

Suddenly the Commvee's side door burst open, and Debbie Thornberry stormed out. In one hand she held the family teapot. In the other, she held up her adopted brother, Donnie, by the back of his pants.

"Bad news," Debbie announced. "Jungle Boy used the teapot to store his grub worms."

Nigel and Cordelia spat out their tea.

Donnie dropped to the ground and began a complicated wiggling dance to fix his wedgie.

Suddenly Eliza and Darwin charged into camp. "Dad! Mom! Stampede!"

"Battle stations, everybody!" Marianne shouted just as a herd of gazelles stampeded through the camp.

"Mumsy," Nigel instructed Cordelia, "stand absolutely still."

Cordelia couldn't have moved if she tried. She was terrified.

Nigel tried to reassure her. "They're not carnivores. In fact, the gazelle is actually quite harmless . . . unless you happen to be a tuft of grass. . . ."

As the last gazelle passed through the camp, Eliza saw why the gazelles were running.

A sleek spotted cheetah ran through the camp. A cheetah Eliza had seen before.

"It's Akela!" Eliza whispered to Darwin.

As the dust settled, Nigel helped his stunned mother into a chair.

Cordelia held her hand to her chest. "Does this sort of thing happen often?"

Eliza and her sister exchanged a look. Then they traded a look with their parents. This sort of thing happened *all* the time. But they didn't want to worry Cordelia.

"Uh, not much," Nigel fudged.

"Not really," Eliza fibbed, crossing her fingers behind her back.

"Nah," Debbie lied.

To change the subject, Marianne began to gather her photography equipment. "Nigel, we need to get some footage before it gets dark," she reminded him.

"Right-o!" Nigel said, helping her load the gear.

Marianne climbed onto the Thornberrys' Congo-Com, a zebra-striped motorcycle with three fat wheels and a sidecar. "Girls, mind your grandmother," she instructed.

"Don't worry," Cordelia said, smiling at her two granddaughters. "The girls and I will have a nice, quiet evening together."

Debbie rolled her eyes as she watched her parents drive off. "Just when we get something cool to drive, I have to be grounded."

"Of course you were grounded," Cordelia said. "I

understand you tied young Donnie to a termite mound while baby-sitting him."

Debbie stuffed her hands into the pockets of her ripped jeans. "Hey, he was happy."

Eliza motioned for Darwin to follow her, and the two began to tiptoe off.

"Eliza!" Cordelia exclaimed. "Where do you think you're going?"

"Just going for a walk, Grandmumsy," Eliza answered politely.

Cordelia looked horrified. "But there are wild animals—"

"It's okay," Eliza called over her shoulder. "I do it all the time!"

Cordelia shook her head as Eliza dashed off, chattering with her pet chimpanzee. "Deborah, does your sister always—"

"Talk like a monkey, dress like a geek?" Debbie shrugged. "You get used to it."

▪   ▪   ▪

Eliza ran through the plains, and her heart soared. She loved this place, with its wide-open spaces where the sky stretched out forever. She never wanted to leave.

"Come on," Eliza urged Darwin as she ran toward an outcropping of rocks. "Akela's cubs must be nearby."

"Oh, great—cheetah cubs," Darwin said nervously. "I'm sure they'd love some chimp-and-dip."

Eliza climbed the formation of rocks that her father had told her were called a *kopje*. On the other side she saw two spotted cubs tussling on the ground like kittens. Kosey and Cacia—cubs she had played with the last time her family had traveled through Tanzania.

Eliza rappelled down the rocks and landed with a thud. "Hey, there!" she called out, brushing herself off as she got to her feet.

The cubs stopped their roughhousing and looked around.

"It's Eliza!" Cacia cried.

Eliza ran to hug her friends. "Oh, you've grown so big!" She stepped back and looked around. "Where's Tally?"

Another cub leaped from behind the rocks. "Here I am!" He ran circles around her in greeting. "You should see me run, Eliza. I'm really fast now!"

"As in . . . able to outrun defenseless chimps?" Darwin asked nervously.

"Don't mind Darwin," Eliza said with a giggle. "Hey, I've got an idea. Let's have a race!"

"Yeah!" Tally said.

But before they could begin, Akela appeared from within the tall grass. "Children," she called out in a warm, silken voice. "It's time for dinner."

Darwin jumped behind Eliza. "Don't look at me!" he yelped. "I'm skin and bones."

But Akela paid no attention to Darwin as her cubs crowded around her.

"Mom, Eliza wants us to race!" Tally exclaimed.

Akela shook her head. "No. The plains are too dangerous for little ones like you."

"But, Akela, I'll be with them," Eliza insisted. She stroked Tally's soft fur. "I'd never let anything happen. You can trust me."

"Please, Mom?" Tally begged. "Please?"

Akela sighed, obviously torn. "All right," she said at last. "But keep an eye on them, Eliza. And"—she warned them sternly—"do not go beyond the acacia tree." Then, as silently as she'd appeared, she disappeared to continue her hunting.

Eliza whooped with joy as she sprinted away. "Hey, slowpokes! I'm winning!"

The cubs raced to catch up with her.

They didn't even notice when they ran past the acacia tree.

But Darwin did. He froze and looked around. "Eliza!" he called nervously. "You're past the acacia tree!"

"Don't worry, Darwin!" she shouted. "We'll be fine!"

After all, it was a beautiful day. The sun was setting.

There wasn't a cloud in the sky. And she was the luckiest girl in the world—a girl who could talk and laugh and run with the animals.

What could possibly go wrong? Eliza thought as she zigzagged through the grass.

And then suddenly she heard something that made her stop in her tracks.

A foreign sound. A horrible sound. A noise made only by man.

Gunfire!

Chapter 2

Bap-bap-bap!

Eliza looked around, confused, as the sound of gunshots sliced through the air.

Darwin and the cubs circled her in panic. Then another sound grew—*whomp-whomp-whomp*—whirring like a giant mechanical insect.

The lights of a helicopter washed over them.

"Run!" Eliza yelled.

She and her friends scattered beneath the chopper's churning blades.

But not Tally. Bathed in the spotlight, he froze in fear as the helicopter bore down on him.

Eliza glanced back over her shoulder as she ran, and she saw a rope ladder drop down from the helicopter. Then a man began to climb down. What's he doing? Eliza wondered.

Holding tightly to the rope ladder with one hand, the man reached down toward the ground with the other. . . .

"Tally!" Eliza gasped.

With little thought for her own safety, Eliza changed course and ran toward Tally. Could she reach him before it was too late?

Eliza saw the man's hand reach down, down . . .

But she scooped up the little cheetah cub just in time. "Tally!" she cried. He was safe!

But then she felt him yanked from her arms. The man grabbed Tally by the scruff of the neck and started up the ladder.

"Eliza! Help!" Tally cried.

Eliza heard a furious growl behind her as Akela hurtled from the darkness and tore into the man's arm, ripping his jacket.

With an angry shout, the man kicked Akela to the ground.

As the helicopter picked up speed Akela quickly jumped to her feet and began to run—so fast Eliza could barely believe her eyes.

But just as Akela reached the dangling rope ladder, the helicopter veered sharply upward to avoid the oncoming *kopje*.

Eliza scrambled up the rock formation. As the rope ladder swept over her, she jumped from the edge and caught the end of it.

Nigel and Marianne had heard the shots and drove up in the Congo-Com just in time to see their daughter leaping through the air ten feet above the plain!

"Eliza!" Marianne cried. She jammed the gas pedal to the floor and jerked the steering wheel hard. Dust flew into the air as she raced after the chopper.

As Eliza struggled to get her footing on the rope ladder, she stared up at the kidnapper. She couldn't see his face because he wore a headlamp strapped around his forehead. She turned away, blinded for a moment by the light. Then she began to climb.

The man seemed stunned by this young girl's unexpected bravery. He watched her climb, pulling herself up with determination. Reaching up, she managed to grab hold of Tally's hind leg.

"Give him back!" Eliza cried. "He's just a baby!"

The man pulled a dagger from the side of his boot. Its curved ivory handle was carved in the shape of a falcon. Its blade glinted as he raised it in the air.

Eliza gasped and slipped, then quickly regained her footing.

Down below, Nigel shouted into his walkie-talkie, "Deborah! We need you to bring the Commvee right away!"

On the other end of the radio, Debbie's voice sounded bored. "I wish I could, Dad, but I'm grounded—remember?"

Marianne snatched the walkie-talkie from Nigel's hand. "Debbie—NOW!"

· · ·

Debbie didn't have to be asked again. Minutes after her mother's command, she was barreling across the plains in the Thornberrys' Commvee.

Beside her, Cordelia Thornberry hung on to her wide-brimmed safari hat and struggled to stay in her seat. "Deborah!" Cordelia scolded. "Slow down immediately!"

"Sorry, Grandmumsy! Mom's orders!"

Just then Donnie climbed onto the dashboard, dancing wildly and blocking Debbie's view.

"This is no time for the wedgie dance!" Debbie hollered. "Will *somebody* do something?"

"'Somebody'?" Cordelia snorted and pulled Donnie into her lap. "We'll discuss your impertinence later, young lady."

"Debbie!" Nigel shouted into his walkie-talkie as the Commvee came into view. "Follow that helicopter!"

Debbie, Cordelia, and Donnie looked up and saw Eliza dangling from the ladder.

Cordelia gasped.

Debbie shifted gears and groaned. "I couldn't have had a sister who plays with dolls."

Suddenly the ladder swung wildly to one side and Eliza screamed. A few rungs above her the man had cut one side of the ladder with his knife. Now he was sawing furiously at the other side.

Quickly Nigel jumped from the sidecar of the Congo-Com to the outside of the moving Commvee. As it bounced along, he carefully inched his way to the door. When he reached the passenger-side window, he stuck his head inside. "Hello, Mumsy. Having a jolly holiday?"

Cordelia snorted in disapproval. "Nigel, we must discuss your children's manners."

"We're equally as proud, Mumsy," Nigel agreed. "But now's not the time." He reached across his mother and yanked a handle.

The roof of the Commvee instantly inflated into a giant cushion—just as the poacher's knife severed the final rope.

"Eliza!" Marianne screamed as she watched her daughter fall.

Debbie stomped on the gas, swerving to position herself directly below her sister.

Boing! Eliza landed on the inflatable roof of the Commvee, bouncing as if she were on a trampoline.

"Can I drive or *what?*" Debbie congratulated herself.

But then the Commvee skidded out of control.

Debbie fought to steady the wheel as the vehicle spun, kicking up a cloud of dirt.

Marianne watched helplessly as Eliza slid toward the edge of the roof.

Debbie pounded the dashboard with her fist, striking a dozen buttons and knobs. Tires squealed as she pulled the Commvee to a stop. Just in time an awning popped out over a window and caught Eliza like a hammock.

She lay there a moment, catching her breath. The only sounds she could hear were the beating of her heart . . . and the fading *whomp-whomp-whomp* of the helicopter as it disappeared into the evening sky.

"Oh, Tally!" Eliza whispered, looking out beyond the circle of her family to search for another mother. . . .

There, amid the moonlit plain, Akela stared into the sky where the helicopter had disappeared.

Only Eliza could understand the words she howled over and over: "My baby . . . my baby . . ."

Tally's gone, Eliza thought. And it's all my fault.

Chapter 3

Eliza and her family had returned to camp. Now that her parents knew she was safe, they quickly remembered how to scold.

Nigel had called in his oldest friend, Chief of Parks, Jomo Mbeli, along with several other park rangers.

"Poachers are dangerous people," Jomo said.

Eliza hung her head.

"Eliza, are you listening?" Marianne asked.

"But the poacher was taking Tally!" Eliza cried.

Marianne looked at her curiously. "Who?"

"Oh. Uh . . . ," Eliza said, thinking fast, "that's what I named the cheetah cub."

Cordelia threw up her hands in amazement. "She *names* man-eating wild animals as if they're pets?"

"Could you identify the poacher, Eliza?" Jomo asked.

Eliza shook her head. "No, he shined a light in my eyes." But then she remembered something that might help. "But I saw his knife!" she said eagerly. "The handle was carved in the shape of a falcon. That will help you find him, won't it?"

Jomo exchanged a look with Nigel, then sighed and shook his head. "There are many knives, many poachers."

"But I have to find Tally!"

"Eliza, you must leave this to us," Jomo insisted, his voice kind but firm. "Promise me you will never go off alone at night."

Eliza dug her toe in the dirt. "I promise," she said, trying to mean it.

Jomo smiled briefly at her parents. "I will call if I hear anything. Good night."

"Thank you, Jomo," Nigel said.

When Jomo drove off, Marianne turned to her youngest daughter. "Eliza, you must keep your promise."

Debbie snickered. "Yeah, right. She and the monkey are always sneaking off—"

"Deb-bie!" Eliza couldn't believe her ears, especially after all that had just happened. She stared into her sister's eyes, begging her not to betray her.

But Debbie's face had hardened into a mask of teenage indifference, and she shrugged. "Hey, I've covered for you long enough." Then she turned to her parents. "Do you know she once fed one of my protein bars to a Komodo dragon?"

Her father's mouth fell open.

"And did you know she rode a Siberian tiger?" Debbie added.

Marianne's face went pale.

Debbie, stop—please?! Eliza pleaded with her eyes.

"Ask her about the time she was dancing with a bunch of crazy dingoes."

Cordelia gasped.

Marianne took Eliza by the shoulders and stared into her eyes. "Eliza, is this true?"

But Eliza just looked away.

Debbie smirked. "That's not even the half of it, Mom."

"Eliza!" Nigel exclaimed, clearly shocked.

"Thanks a lot, Deb." Eliza shot her sister a look that would make a herd of wildebeest retreat. But Debbie just ignored her.

Marianne sagged against her husband. "Nigel, I-I don't know what to do."

"Well, I do!" Cordelia Thornberry marched over to admonish her son. "It is perfectly obvious that Elizabeth has no regard for her own personal safety. We have discussed this for years. She needs to be in a structured environment—one such as boarding school back in London."

"What?!" Eliza cried.

"Oh, hold on," Debbie protested. "*She* messes up . . . and *she* gets to go to a luxurious boarding school?"

"Mumsy," Nigel said, "that's rather drastic."

"Nigel," Cornelia replied sharply, "need I remind you that it was in the confines of boarding school that *you* received *your* education, not here in the wild? Surely you don't think it's civilized for a girl to play with cheetahs and chimps?"

Debbie leaped onto the picnic table. "Hello? What about *me?* Eep! Eeep! Ooh! Ooh! Ooh!" She pounded her chest like a gorilla. "See?" she asked her grandmother. "Do I look civilized?"

Cordelia gave her a look. "Frankly, no. But I am afraid it's much too late for you, dear."

Debbie wailed and buried her face in her hands.

"This isn't about being civilized, Debbie," Marianne said. She laid a hand on her youngest daughter, her eyes a mixture of love and fear. "Eliza, we just can't have you going up against men with guns."

"But who's going to save Tally?" Eliza cried.

"Honey, you have to let Jomo handle that," Marianne said.

"Dad, please . . ."

"Poppet, your intentions are noble," Nigel said

with a catch in his throat. "But you're just too young. I'm sorry."

Eliza's heart sank. Even Dad is against me? she wondered. Without a word, she ran to the tent that she and Darwin shared.

Maybe if she went to sleep she could wake up and discover that this was all just a bad dream.

Chapter 4

Inside the Commvee, Nigel and Marianne were unusually quiet as they got ready for bed. Marianne perched on the edge, studying a framed photo. It was one of her favorites—a picture of her family taken about four years ago, standing in front of an ordinary suburban house. That life seemed worlds away, and she couldn't imagine going back.

She and Nigel were doing important work. Living their dream. Using their talents to help educate people and save the animals of the world. She'd always believed it was a good way to raise her children, too.

But now she wasn't so sure.

"We agreed when we took this job that we wouldn't split up the family," she said sadly. "We'd keep the children with us, on the road. . . ."

"I remember, dearest," Nigel said softly.

Marianne set the photo on the nightstand and climbed into bed. "Oh, Nigel!" she exclaimed. "Are we doing the right thing?"

Nigel slipped his arm around his wife's shoulders. "It's our only choice, dearest. Eliza is not going to listen to reason when it comes to traipsing off into the wild. She's quite fearless, you know."

Marianne's eyes glistened with tears as she gave him a small smile. "She takes after her father."

Nigel smiled sadly, then turned out the light. But it was a long time before either one slept, for neither wanted to see the sun rise on the day they would send their daughter away.

■　　■　　■

Cordelia couldn't sleep, so she got up to make a cup of tea. As she waited for the water to boil, she heard a strange sound coming from outside.

Uneasy, she raised the window and looked out.

A strange chittering sound came from Eliza's tent.

She's talking monkey-talk with that silly chimp again, Cordelia thought in disapproval. She couldn't believe Marianne let her granddaughter sleep with a wild animal as if it were a neatly groomed house pet. Why, it probably had fleas or . . . or some strange jungle disease. Goodness, what would the Queen think?

With a snort, Cordelia closed the window. Tomorrow she would rescue her granddaughter from this horrid wilderness—as any good grand-mother would do.

And from the looks of things, it couldn't be a moment too soon.

* * *

In their small tent Eliza and Darwin whispered like two kids staying up late at a sleepover. They sat on their sleeping bags with an electric lantern between them.

Eliza had just explained her grandmother's plans.

"Boarding school?!" Darwin exclaimed. "I never heard of anything so ridiculous!" He fluffed his pillow and turned over on his back. "Did anyone bother to ask *my* opinion?"

Eliza sighed. "Sometimes I wish I could just tell them I can talk to animals. . . ."

Darwin bolted upright. "No!" he said frantically. "Then you'll lose your power! And we'll never be able to talk again! How will I know what Debbie is saying about me?!"

"Calm down, I won't break the rule," Eliza assured him. "I promised Shaman Mnyambo."

"Good." Darwin crossed his arms and sighed in relief. "Now, about this boarding school—you don't think they'll make me take gym class, do you? Because those tight shorts show off my problem area." He motioned to his backside.

Eliza gulped. How can I tell him? she thought. There was no easy way. Best just get it over with. "Um, Darwin . . . ," she began.

He looked at her expectantly.

She took a deep breath and blurted out: "You can't come with me."

Darwin stared at her a moment as if she'd suddenly lost her ability to speak to animals. As if he couldn't understand a word she'd said.

Then he bolted from the tent, his shrieks echoing through the night as he fled into the jungle.

"Darwin!" Eliza dashed out of the tent to stop him, and nearly ran into her father, who'd just stepped out of the Commvee in his bathrobe.

"Whatever is wrong with Darwin?" Nigel asked.

Eliza sighed. "Um, I guess he saw me pack my suitcase."

Nigel nodded. "Very intuitive, that chimp. It's as if he *knows* you'll be thousands of miles away, and we'll be deep in the jungle, cut off from radio communication for weeks—" Her father's voice broke with emotion and he began to cry. "I don't know how he'll stand it!"

Eliza choked back a sob. She hated to see her father cry. It made his mustache soggy. She gave him her handkerchief.

31

Nigel loudly blew his nose, then tucked the hankie into his own pocket.

"What are you doing up, Dad?" Eliza asked.

"Oh, I couldn't sleep, so I thought I would plot our course through the Congo." He held up a rolled-up map. "We are hoping to film the elusive forest elephants."

Nigel carried the map to the picnic table and unrolled it.

Eliza put rocks on the corners of the map to keep the edges from curling up. "Why are the elephants so hard to find?"

"Well, partly because of the dense jungle, and partly because they have been hunted almost to extinction," Nigel explained. "Their tusks yield what's known as 'rose ivory'—a favorite of poachers."

Eliza stared at her clenched fists. "I hate poachers."

"Still thinking of that young cheetah, aren't you?" her father asked softly.

Eliza nodded.

Nigel patted her on the shoulder. "Don't lose heart, Eliza. I'll keep an eye out."

"Thanks, Dad." But it was too sad to think about, so she quickly changed the subject. "Mom said you were filming an eclipse."

"Oh, yes, that's part of it." He turned back to his map. "You see, there's a BaAka legend that when a solar eclipse occurs in the Tembo Valley, thousands of elephants gather and stand in silence as the moon obscures the sun."

"I wonder why they do it?" Eliza said.

Her father shrugged. "Nobody knows. The last eclipse in this area was more than two hundred years ago. But when the eclipse occurs this time"— he gazed up at the almost full moon—"I plan to be there."

"I wish *I* could be there, Dad," Eliza said wistfully.

Nigel looked as if he were about to cry again. With a sniffle, he removed the necklace he wore.

He held it out for Eliza to see. A small, round medal dangled from the chain.

"I received this medal when I was in boarding school," he explained. "I was about your age. Perhaps you would like to take it . . . for luck." He pressed the medal into her hand.

Eliza read the engraved words aloud. "'Awarded for bravery.'" She looked up at her father in surprise.

Nigel blushed. "Oh, there was an incident with the coal bin . . . a small fire. Nothing really. We were trapped on the tenth floor, and I constructed a rope bridge . . . well, never mind. The point is, you will have your own challenges, poppet. And I predict you will meet them splendidly."

Eliza's eyes blurred with tears. She didn't want to

go away. She didn't want to leave her father and his wonderful work with animals.

But if she had to go, she would do everything she could to live up to his example. To make him proud.

She slipped the medal over her head, then threw her arms around her father.

●　　●　　●

When morning came, Eliza tried not to wake up. She squeezed her eyes shut, trying to make herself fall back asleep, trying to keep the day from beginning.

She rolled over and reached for Darwin's hand.

But his sleeping bag was empty.

Eliza sat up with a start. Darwin never came back! Her heart sank as she realized she wouldn't even get a chance to say good-bye to her best friend.

Nobody spoke much at breakfast—not even Debbie. Eliza's father tried to be his usual cheerful self, but his voice kept trailing off. . . . Her mom was crying into the pancake batter. Debbie kept her nose buried in a Des Brodean fan magazine, and Marianne didn't even scold Debbie for reading at the table. Cordelia tried to start a polite conversation about the weather, but even she gave up.

At last they all piled into the Commvee, and Marianne drove them to a small airport in Tanzania.

A six-seater Cessna airplane waited on the dirt airstrip.

As the pilot loaded the luggage, he struggled a little with the weight of Eliza's duffel bag.

"My sister's a major nature geek," Debbie confided to the pilot. "She probably packed her rock collection."

Then she strode up to Eliza and held out a long list. "Here's what I need you to get me in London," she announced. "CDs, boots, T-shirts—basically, *anything* cool." She thrust the list into Eliza's hands.

Eliza took it without a word, and Debbie stepped back.

But Marianne gave her oldest daughter a nudge.

With a sigh, Debbie gave Eliza a limp hug. "Don't forget," she whispered. *"Cool."*

"Well, all set," Marianne said with forced cheer as she led Eliza toward the plane. "I packed your blue sweater in case it gets chilly, and peanut-butter cookies, in case you get homesick—uh, *hungry* . . . in case you get *hungry.* Uh, now, remember to call the very minute you get there—" And then she choked back a sob.

Eliza hugged her tight. "Thanks, Mom."

"Remember," Marianne said, overcome with emotion, "you have something to offer your new classmates. Just be yourself. It's going to be a great experience." She smiled, holding back her tears, then managed to say, "I love you."

Cordelia bustled up and took Eliza under her wing.

"Now, don't fret about Eliza," she said briskly. "I'll check on her once a week." She quickly hugged Marianne, Debbie, and Nigel, then headed for the plane.

Eliza hugged Donnie, and he slipped a dung beetle into her backpack as she turned to her father. "You won't leave without Darwin, will you, Dad?"

"We'll find him, poppet," her father promised.

"Elizabeth!" Cordelia called from the doorway of the plane. She was now wearing goggles and a long aviator scarf. "It's time for takeoff! Kiss your natural wilderness girlhood good-bye!"

"Heavens, Mumsy!" Nigel exclaimed. "Are you flying the plane?"

"Don't be silly," Cordelia replied. "I know nothing about flying. I'm just going to sit next to the pilot and make sure he does everything correctly."

Nigel gave his daughter one final encouraging smile and a thumbs-up, then shut the door behind her.

The Cessna roared to life, then taxied down the dusty runway.

Nigel held Marianne in his arms they watched the

plane take off. "Don't cry, dear. Every hatchling must one day leave the nest."

⬛ ⬛ ⬛

Up in the sky Eliza pressed her forehead against the window, gazing one last time at the land she loved.

She saw zebras cantering across the plains. A river teeming with bathing hippos. A pride of lions sunning themselves on a *kopje*. A flock of flamingoes flying in a V-formation with slow, lazy wing beats.

All I ever wanted to do was travel the world and meet the animals, she thought as a tear trickled down her cheek.

But now her adventures were over . . . forever.

London, England

Eliza peered through the wrought-iron gates of Lady Beatrice's School for Girls.

A gaggle of schoolgirls gathered around a flagpole as the British flag was being raised. Their identical crimson blazers, skirts, and caps as well as their excited chatter made Eliza think of a flock of birds she'd once seen in South America.

And now I'm one of them, she thought miserably, glancing down at her own crimson uniform. But she felt like the odd duck out.

Cordelia Thornberry straightened her grand-daughter's hat. "Remember, dear, I'm on the board of directors. Do me proud!"

Eliza tried to smile.

Cordelia gave her a quick hug, then popped into the back seat of her chauffeur-driven car and drove off.

Eliza gulped and turned back to face the school.

She clasped the medal she wore around her neck. Her father's medal.

I'm Nigel Thornberry's daughter, she thought. I've faced lions and tigers and gorillas. I can do this. With a deep breath, she hoisted her backpack on one shoulder and marched through the gates, rolling her wheeled duffel bag behind her along the cobblestone drive.

As she headed for the headmistress's office, she felt everyone staring.

Suddenly the wheels of Eliza's duffel caught on one of the cobblestones, jerking her backward so that she tripped and fell. Her backpack flew from her shoulder, and its contents spilled out across the courtyard: a canteen, exotic feathers, a compass, binoculars . . .

The girls pointed and whispered and giggled. Someone squealed when Donnie's huge dung beetle scurried through the pile.

Embarrassed, Eliza began to gather up her things. No one offered to help.

Funny, she thought. She would run with Darwin deep into the jungle or across the wide-open plains without another human in sight, and she never felt alone.

But here, in the middle of a crowded city, surrounded by girls her own age, Eliza felt totally alone.

* * *

Eliza opened the door to her dorm room and peeked inside. The room was small but nice, with two single beds, two dressers, a tall wardrobe, and a mirror.

I wonder what my roommate will be like, Eliza thought as she shrugged out of her jacket and tossed her hat on the dresser. She pulled a framed picture from her backpack and placed it on her nightstand: a photo of her family in Africa, with Darwin in the middle. She tried not to think about what they might be doing right now.

Had they found Darwin? Was he all right?

Sighing, she dragged her heavy duffel bag across the floor and heaved it onto the bed.

She jumped back.

The bag seemed to be . . . wiggling.

Eliza leaned forward and gasped when she heard muffled noises coming from inside the bag!

"That's it! One more bump and you'll have scrambled chimp!" a voice said.

The bag ripped open and Darwin popped out, gasping for air.

"Darwin!" Eliza sprang forward to hug him.

"You didn't think I would let *you* get civilized without *me,* did you?" he said.

40

"It's so great to see you!" Then Eliza rushed to lock the door. "But you can't be here!"

"Yes, it's a miracle I survived the baggage hold."

Eliza shook her head. "No, Darwin—I *told* you, they don't allow chimps at boarding school!"

Darwin just chuckled. "Oh, they'll change their minds when they meet *me*. Now, let's take a look at my new home." He stood on the bed and surveyed the room. "Small, yet charming. Not much in the way of natural light, but haven't we really had enough of nature? Oh—dibs on that bed!"

He flounced onto the other bed and began to jump up and down. "Oooh, feel these springs!" he exclaimed in delight. "Firm, yet flexible. Come on, Eliza, try it!"

Eliza giggled—she couldn't help herself.

But then she froze. Someone was out in the hall, jiggling the doorknob—trying to enter the room!

"Oh, no! Someone's coming!" Eliza whispered frantically.

"Room service?" Darwin jumped off the bed and ran to the door. "Oh, I like school already!"

Frantically Eliza grabbed Darwin and stuffed him under the bed. "Shhh! Darwin, no!" she whispered.

Knock—knock—knock!

The pounding on the door grew louder.

"Uh, just a minute!" Eliza called out.

41

"Let me in!" a girl shouted through the door.

Under the bed was too risky, Eliza decided. "Quick! In here!" She gently shoved Darwin into the tall wardrobe and closed the door.

"Oooh, stupid key . . . ," the girl outside complained.

Eliza took a deep breath, then flung open the door—just as a blond girl tumbled through the door to the floor. The girl glared up at Eliza.

Eliza smiled and prayed that Darwin would stay put in the wardrobe. "Hi! I'm Eliza Thornberry. Guess we're roommates."

"So it appears." The girl got to her feet and breezed past Eliza as if she owned the room.

"I'm Sarah Wellington," she announced without a trace of a smile. "Have you been romping on my bed?"

Oops. Eliza smiled apologetically as she rushed to smooth the spread. "Oh, just trying out the springs—firm, yet flexible!"

Sarah folded her arms and scowled. "Perhaps we should take this opportunity to negotiate a few issues," she said. "You stay on your side of the room, and I stay on mine."

She marched over to her dresser, on which she'd carefully arranged an elegant silver brush and comb set, hand mirror, and crystal perfume bottle. "My things shall be off limits, as they are antique and rather expensive. This perfume is French. And don't even dream about wearing my clothes. . . ."

Great, Eliza thought miserably. This is like having Debbie for a roommate!

Suddenly Sarah frowned, and Eliza followed her gaze to the wardrobe, which was standing ajar. "A-ha! I see that you have already rooted through my wardrobe!"

Oh, no! Eliza looked around for something to distract her roommate—and spotted the cookie tin her mother had tucked into her duffel bag.

"Sarah!" Eliza exclaimed. "Want one of my mom's homemade peanut-butter cookies?"

Sarah stopped in her tracks and turned around, a greedy look on her face.

Behind her, Eliza could see Darwin. He was inside the wardrobe, wearing a raincoat and hanging from the clothes rod. Her hand shook as she shoved the cookie tin into Sarah's eager hands. Then she shut the wardrobe again, leaning back against the door to keep it closed.

"I might have a use for you yet," Sarah said as she eagerly ripped open the tin.

Then she scowled.

The tin held nothing but a few crumbs.

Disgusted, Sarah shoved the tin back into Eliza's hands. "Very funny."

Darwin let out a huge burp from inside the wardrobe.

To cover up, Eliza pretended she did it. "Uh, excuse me!"

Eliza sighed. So much for making new friends. . . .

* * *

At dinner that night Eliza sat alone at one of the long tables in the dining room. All around her, girls talked and laughed. They all seemed to be the best of friends.

Eliza felt invisible.

She nibbled at her food, but sneaked most of it into her pockets. As soon as she could, she excused herself and hurried upstairs to her room.

Once inside, she closed the door and leaned against it, relieved to be alone. But then she spotted a certain chimp brushing his hair with Sarah's antique silver brush! "Darwin!" Eliza cried.

She quickly took the brush away and handed Darwin the food she'd brought him. "How am I ever going to keep you a secret?" Eliza said as she watched Darwin scarf down shepherd's pie, rolls, and fruit. She dabbed at his milk-mustache with a napkin.

When the phone rang, Eliza leaped to answer it. "Hello?"

"Eliza? Can you hear me? It's Mom!"

"And your dear old dad!"

The line was full of static, but Eliza thought her parents sounded wonderful.

"How's school?" her mom asked.

"Yes, how are things in old England?" her father shouted. "What I'd give for a good cuppa!"

"Yeah, like she can even appreciate whatever that is," Eliza heard her sister complain in the background.

"Debbie, please," Marianne said, "I can't hear Eliza."

"Has Jomo found Tally yet?" Eliza asked.

"Sorry, poppet," Nigel replied. "In fact, the poachers disappeared without a trace."

"Nigel," she heard her mother whisper. "Tell her about Darwin."

"Yes, I was leading up to that." Nigel cleared his throat, obviously struggling to find the right words. "Poodles," he said gently, "I'm afraid we've lost track of Darwin."

Eliza's heart twisted as she watched the "missing chimp" who was right in front of her. She hated keeping things from her parents.

"I'm sure he's fine," Eliza said. "He's probably

stuffing his face right now. You know Darwin."

At the mention of his name, Darwin looked up. "This shepherd's pie is heavenly! But why did they put these mushy green things in it? They look like bunny droppings!"

"Honey," Marianne asked. "Is someone there?"

"Oh! That's, uh . . . Regina," Eliza fibbed.

"She sounds delightful!" Nigel exclaimed. "And hungry. Give your new best friend our best, would you?"

"She's making *friends?*" Debbie squawked in the background. "Give me that!"

Debbie came on the line. "Here's what's going on in *my* life," she wailed. "Donnie is now half-goat, my hair is half-terrier, and we're heading into the abyss where there is no hope of teen interaction. Good-bye!"

With that, she slammed down the phone.

Eliza shook her head. At least everything back home was the same as usual.

- - -

The days crawled by. Eliza was exhausted from trying to hide Darwin. She didn't talk much to the other girls because she was so worried about getting caught. And she grew more and more homesick every day.

At least I've made a few friends, she thought as she sat on a bench feeding peanuts to the squirrels.

"Thanks," one of the squirrels said. "Can't get enough of these nuts."

Eliza sighed. "It's so great to talk to you guys. You have no idea how awful it's been here."

The squirrels stuffed their cheeks.

A large squirrel named Reggie glanced at the others in disgust. "Go on, Eliza. Tell Reggie your troubles. Uh, before you do, I don't suppose you have any of those cheesy snacks I fancy?"

"Cheese Munchies?" Eliza smiled and pulled a bag from her pocket. "Here."

"Much obliged," Reggie said with his mouth full. "Now, what's the problem?"

Eliza shrugged. "I just miss my friends in Africa. Oh, you should see it there, Reggie. I've even met some squirrels who fly."

"Fly? Like birds?" he exclaimed. "Hmm. Don't like the sound of that."

Across the campus Sarah and her friends Jane and Victoria stopped to stare at Eliza. When they heard her making squirrel noises, they quickly turned away.

"I heard that her family lives in the jungle in a motor home," Victoria said.

"And that she bathes where animals drink!" Sarah added.

"*Ewwww!*" Jane and Victoria squealed.

"Next she'll be bringing animals into the room," Sarah said, leading her friends away.

• • •

The next night at dinner Mrs. Fairgood, the headmistress, stood at the front of the cafeteria, holding a small bell. "Proper posture, girls!" she called out as the girls took their places and stood straight behind their chairs. Satisfied, Mrs. Fairgood rang the bell, and the girls quickly pulled back their chairs and sat down to eat.

Eliza was surprised when Victoria and Jane slid into seats near her.

"We're a little curious," Victoria said, her eyes bright and inquisitive. "Have you ever seen a tiger up close?"

"Actually, I have seen lots of tigers," Eliza said. "And Komodo dragons, and lions, and bears."

The girls gasped, clearly impressed, and leaned forward to hear more.

"Once, when we were in the Arctic, I hung out with a polar bear," Eliza went on. "They're really playful."

The girls giggled, but Eliza realized they weren't teasing or making fun of her. They were listening. They were really interested! Could she make some friends after all?

"And then there was the humpback whale in Hawaii," Eliza went on. "I swam right next to him. They're amazing animals. They're really gentle, and they make these sounds that are like songs. . . ."

Eliza didn't notice, but Sarah was watching her from a distance with a frown on her face. "It seems my roommate is making friends," she muttered. "*My* friends!" She quickly got her food and marched over to the table, where she plunked her tray down right in front of Eliza.

"Sarah," Jane said excitedly. "Eliza swam with the whales!"

"Isn't that lovely," Sarah replied flatly.

"Tell us more, Eliza!" Victoria begged.

"Did you see any sharks?"

"Was the water cold?"

"What was it like?"

The questions came rapid-fire from all sides. Eliza was so busy answering questions, she didn't notice when a chubby girl flopped down in the chair next to her.

The girl tugged at Eliza's sleeve until she turned around.

Eliza's mouth fell open in surprise.

The chubby girl had the school cap pulled way down over her head, but Eliza could still see her hair—lots of it.

"Darwin?" she whispered.

The chimp looked up coyly and nodded. "Don't I look fetching?" he whispered back.

Shocked, Eliza turned back to the other girls, trying to block their view of her best friend.

"Where was I? Oh, yeah. Swimming with the dingoes—I mean, *dolphins!* But enough about me! Did anyone try the boiled cabbage? I can't get enough boiled cabbage! I'm going back for seconds! Anyone else?"

She stood up abruptly, gesturing behind her for Darwin to stand up and follow her.

But he was too busy eating to notice.

The other girls tried to look around Eliza, curious about their new classmate.

"Who's that girl?" Jane asked.

"I've never seen her before," Victoria replied.

"She's rather plain," one girl whispered.

"She's eating with her fingers!" another girl shrieked.

Eliza tugged on Darwin's blazer, trying to get him to follow her. That's when she noticed the initials S.W. embroidered on the pocket.

Sarah Wellington jumped to her feet and pointed an accusing finger. "That's *my* monogram!" she cried. "Who are you, and why are you wearing my new blazer!"

She ran around and began to tug on her blazer—
and gasped when she revealed Darwin's *very* hairy
arm.

When Darwin tugged back, his cap fell off.

Sarah screamed.

Darwin screamed back, hopped onto the table-
top, and ran through the plates and bowls of food
to the end of the long table.

"No, Darwin, no!" Eliza shouted.

"It's a chimpanzee!" someone shrieked.

The room erupted. Everyone was laughing or
screaming—or both.

"This is the best dinner we ever had!" Victoria
shouted, and all the other girls agreed.

But Mrs. Fairgood did not.

·   ·   ·

After a strong lecture, Mrs. Fairgood led Eliza
and Darwin to the school's stables. Animals were
not allowed in any of the girls' rooms, she
informed Eliza, so Darwin would have to stay in a
horse stall for the night.

"Miss Thornberry," she said, her voice dripping
with disapproval, "your grandmother will be here in
the morning, and when we revive her, I am sure she'll
be gravely disappointed. Now come along!" She
swept outside and waited for Eliza to follow.

"Eliza!" Darwin begged. "Please don't leave me in this place. I'll never last the night!"

Then he noticed the horse who was sharing his stall. "No offense. I'm sure you're very nice. 'Thunder,' is it? How horsey. . . ."

Eliza could see that Mrs. Fairgood was getting impatient, so she gave Darwin a quick hug. "I'll see you in the morning, Dar."

"Trot along, lassie," the big black horse said in a thick Scottish accent. "Your friend will be fine with me."

"Thanks, Thunder."

"Miss Thornberry!" Mrs. Fairgood called sharply. "I said, come along!"

Resigned to his fate, Darwin gazed up at his tall four-legged roommate. "I could use a hot bath and a good meal."

Thunder tossed his mane, pointing to the nearest feeding trough. "You're in luck. They'll be bringing the hay around any minute."

Darwin's face twisted in disgust. "I'm to eat *hay?*"

"Aye, and sweet and crunchy oats from time to time too," Thunder replied.

"Oh, that changes everything," Darwin said sarcastically. "Never mind. Where's the bathroom?"

Thunder scuffed the thick layer of hay spread out along the barn floor with his hoof. "You're standing on it."

"No, really," Darwin said. "Where's the—" Then he stopped, wide-eyed, and lifted his feet off the hay as he suddenly understood what Thunder meant.

Crossing the courtyard behind Mrs. Fairgood, Eliza heard Darwin's high-pitched shriek: "ELIZA!!!"

• • •

Alone in her room, Eliza changed into her pj's and curled up on her bed. She picked up the photo of her family and sighed. I'm not exactly living up to Dad's example, she thought miserably. She'd been here only a short while, and already she was in trouble.

A soft knock at the door interrupted her thoughts, and Victoria poked her head in. "Eliza? May we come in?"

Victoria opened the door, and much to Eliza's surprise, Jane and several other girls dressed in their nightclothes swarmed into the room. They plopped onto her bed and bombarded her with excited questions.

"How is the chimp?"

"Did Mrs. Fairgood make him go to the zoo?"

"How did you hide him from Sarah?"

"Girls! Girls! Settle down!" Jane said in a perfect imitation of Mrs. Fairgood's voice as everyone laughed.

"Eliza, tell us *everything*," Jane begged. "However did you smuggle the chimp in your suitcase?"

"I didn't," Eliza admitted. "Darwin decided to—" She caught herself just in time. She couldn't tell these girls that she had real conversations with Darwin. "I mean, um, that was easy. Hiding him from Sarah, that's a different story."

Victoria huffed. "Oh, Miss Wellington thinks she's the bee's knees," she said, and several of the girls murmured their agreement.

"Tell us more about the wild animals," Victoria begged.

"Yes, it sounds so exotic!" Jane exclaimed. "Why would you ever come here where it's so boring?"

"I got into trouble," Eliza explained. "I snuck out at night, and there were poachers—"

"Poachers!"

"With guns?"

"What happened?"

"Were you scared?"

Eliza wrapped her arms around her knees and took a deep breath. As the memories came flooding back, she got a faraway look in her eyes. "There were these three cheetah cubs I knew," she began. "They're like kittens, only wild. We were running when we heard shots. Someone was trying to shoot their mother."

The girls gasped, listening breathlessly.

"A man dropped out of a helicopter on a rope ladder and grabbed the one I named Tally," Eliza went on. "I tried to save him, but the man cut the ladder and I fell. . . ." She looked around at her friends, her eyes filling with tears. "And Tally was gone."

"Poor Tally," Jane said softly.

"I think he's alive," Eliza said. "I just feel it."

"This is terrible!" Victoria exclaimed. "Can't we write letters or something?"

"Let's have a bake sale!" Jane suggested.

And suddenly all the girls were talking at once:

"Yes, let's!"

"We have to save Tally!"

"What can we do, Eliza?"

Eliza looked around at all her new friends, and she felt happy for the first time since she'd come to Lady Beatrice's school. But a bake sale wouldn't do much. "Thanks, you guys. But I don't think—"

"What's going on in my room," a shrill voice demanded, "and why wasn't I invited?"

Sarah stood in the open doorway in an expensive-looking robe and pajamas, scowling at them all.

"Sarah," Jane said, "Eliza was just telling us the most awful story, about Tally—"

"Never mind," Sarah said coldly. "I have been at Mrs. Fairgood's, filling out a report, and I'm quite tired. You'll all have to go now."

Reluctantly the girls filed out of the room.

Eliza slipped under her covers.

As Sarah got into bed, she muttered, "I still can't believe you harbored a wild animal in my room, and I never saw—AAAGGHHHHHH!!!"

Sarah threw back her covers and stared at her feet. "There are *peas* in my bed! Someone's been eating in my bed!"

Eliza pulled the covers over her head.

·   ·   ·

Rain drummed on the windowpanes of Lady Beatrice's school. The halls were silent as all the girls slept, dreaming of homework, or friends . . . or in Eliza's case, animals running free across the African plains. She tossed and turned.

In her dream, Eliza tiptoed down the quiet hall.

Suddenly an elephant ran through the archway at the entrance to the school!

Eliza rubbed her eyes. What was an elephant doing in London, at a girls' school? Had it escaped from the zoo?

The elephant looked back at Eliza, silently urging her to follow. Mesmerized, Eliza followed the elephant through the archway and found herself . . .

On the savanna, with the sun blazing down on her. She shaded her eyes with her hand as she gazed out across the plain.

Then she spotted something up ahead. Something moving in the thick, swaying grasses.

Eliza ran toward it.

And then she saw that it was Tally, zigzagging through the grass. Suddenly he stopped and gazed back at her.

"Tally!" Eliza shouted. "I knew you were alive!"

Then Eliza saw her family's Commvee fly through the air, with her father standing on the roof.

"Dad!" she shouted. "Tally's alive!"

"That's wonderful, poppet!" her father called back cheerfully.

"Eliza! Help!" Tally cried.

Eliza spun around. An invisible force was pulling Tally into the sky, higher and higher, toward the blazing hot sun.

"No!" Eliza screamed.

And then something blocked the sunlight, and a shadow fell across Eliza's path.

The shadow of Shaman Mnyambo.

"Shaman Mnyambo?" Eliza said. The man she had once saved from a horrible fate as a warthog. The man who had rewarded her by giving her the power to talk to animals. She'd thought she would never see him again.

He spoke to her, his voice deep and dreamlike:

"Tally is only part of the problem. You have a greater destiny, Eliza. You must go to it."

"What do you mean?" she asked.

"Go, Eliza. Go! *Go!*"

She took a step forward—

And screamed as she was sucked down a dark, cavernous hole.

Falling, falling, falling . . .

Chapter 6

Eliza bolted upright, screaming.

Then a light came on.

A very sleepy Sarah had turned on the bedside lamp and was now glaring at her screaming roommate.

And Eliza realized: I'm not in Africa. I didn't fall down a big dark hole. I'm in bed—in England! I must have been dreaming.

This was no ordinary dream. It was a sign.

"Tally's alive," Eliza said, throwing back her covers and leaping out of bed. She knew what she had to do.

She pulled her duffel bag out from under the bed and began to pack.

Sarah gasped. "What are you doing?"

"I have to leave," Eliza said, stuffing clothes and books into her bag.

"I'm calling Mrs. Fairgood," Sarah said as she jumped out of bed and headed for the door.

Eliza blocked her path. "No! Please, you have to keep this a secret. Do you have a credit card? I need two tickets to Africa."

"Africa?!" Sarah stared at Eliza as if she'd lost her mind. "I am *not* taking part in this!"

"My parents will pay you back, I promise," Eliza begged. "And no one will ever know you helped me until it's all over."

"Until what's all over? You're acting so odd. I'm reporting you at once."

"Sarah, please. It's a matter of life and death! I have to go now, and I really need your help. Please."

Sarah folded her arms across her chest.

Eliza had to think quick. "And . . . you'll get the room all to yourself again."

Instantly Sarah picked up the phone. "Would you prefer aisle or window?"

■   ■   ■

Minutes later Eliza raced into the dark stables. "Darwin! Wake up!"

Darwin jumped to his feet. "Eliza, you've come," he said dramatically. "I've tried to keep track of the days, but they blurred into months."

"Dar, it's only been four hours." She grabbed his hand, and they fled into the night.

As they hurried through the streets of London,

Darwin quickly buttoned up his crimson blazer and pulled the cap over his head as a disguise. They raced down the steps to the underground train, then scrambled into a waiting train just before the doors whooshed closed.

Soon they arrived at Heathrow Airport, and Eliza nervously slipped two passports across the counter to the customs officer.

The man flipped one open, glancing at Eliza to check her face against the picture on the passport, then stamped the passport and nodded for her to pass through.

Then he opened the second passport. Sarah Wellington's face smiled back from the picture. When the man glanced up, Darwin hid his face.

The man paused a moment, then stamped the passport as Eliza dragged Darwin through the gate.

Soon they were seated safely in the first-class cabin of the plane. Darwin took the window seat, and Eliza buckled his seat belt.

Darwin twisted and turned in his seat. "Well, it's certainly better than riding in the baggage hold, but I still don't understand why—"

"Shhh! " Eliza warned. "I'll tell you after the plane takes off. I can't risk anyone finding us now."

As the plane took off, Darwin shrieked and leaped up in his seat, accidentally hitting the overhead call button. Immediately a young flight attendant hurried over to ask how she could help.

"Stop fidgeting, Darwin!" Eliza whispered.

"I can't help it." He pulled a clump of straw from his waistband. "I've got hay in my skirt!"

Eliza noticed the flight attendant staring at Darwin. "She has that hairy disease," she explained quickly. "We're going to see a special doctor in Nairobi."

The flight attendant smiled uncertainly and backed away.

Darwin pulled out a sleep mask with the initials S. W. embroidered on it, and slipped it over his eyes.

■　　■　　■

Several hours later the plane touched down in Nairobi, Kenya. Eliza and Darwin quickly slipped onto the last car of a cross-country train. Darwin found a blanket in the overhead bin and tried to get comfortable.

As the train jerked along, Eliza pressed her face to the window and stared at Mt. Kilimanjaro rising majestically in the night sky.

"I'll find you, Tally . . . ," she whispered. "I promise."

With a sigh, she leaned against Darwin, and he spread the blanket out over them both. They were soon rocked to sleep by the moving train.

Masai Mara National Park

Sometime later Eliza was awakened by a strange mournful sound.

An animal—in pain. But where?

She rubbed the sleep from her eyes and looked around.

"Help!" a voice cried from outside the moving train. "The Evil Ones! They're after me!"

Eliza looked out the window.

A large black rhino charged alongside the train. Eliza knew black rhinos could run fast, but even so, his speed amazed her. Especially when she realized—he was bleeding from the neck!

"The Evil Ones . . . ," the rhino moaned.

"Darwin!" Eliza whispered. "Wake up!"

"Huh? What?"

Eliza motioned for Darwin to follow her. Then she rushed out of the compartment into the packed hallway. "Excuse me . . . ," she said, trying to push through the crowd. "Excuse me. . . ."

Darwin followed her, chittering in protest.

At last Eliza reached a coupling between the engineer's car and the passenger car. She stared at the fast-moving ground beneath it. She needed to reach the engineer. She needed to make him stop the train!

Darwin tried to pull her back. "Eliza, no! You won't make it!" He closed his eyes as she leaped to the engineer's car.

She tried the door. But it was locked.

"Let me in!" she cried, pounding on the door. "A rhino's been injured! You have to let me off this train!"

But the engineer couldn't hear her over the noisy clacking of the train wheels along the track.

Eliza turned around. There was a determined look on her face.

Darwin yelped. Oh, no! He could see it in her face. She was going to jump from the moving train!

Eliza took a deep breath and jumped just as the train slowed. She tucked herself into a tight ball and rolled as she hit the ground.

With a nervous shriek, Darwin jumped after her.

As the train picked up speed and rumbled past, Eliza and Darwin scrambled to their feet, a little bruised, but unhurt.

Not far behind them, Eliza spotted the black rhino. Exhausted, he had collapsed to the ground.

Eliza ran and fell to her knees at the injured animal's side. His body heaved as he breathed, obviously in pain.

"Hang on!" Eliza said, running a gentle hand along his head. "We'll get help! You'll be okay!"

Eliza's adventure began on the Serengeti Plain. . . .

She was happily playing with her cheetah cub friend, Tally, and his sisters.

"Give him back! He's just a baby!"

To keep her out of danger, Eliza's parents decided to send her to boarding school in England . . .

. . . where her friend, Darwin, surprised her! "It's so great to see you!" said Eliza. "You didn't think I would let *you* get civilized without *me*, did you?" said Darwin.

Food fight!

In a dream, Eliza realized she had a greater destiny . . . and it was back in Africa! After, her roommate bought her and Darwin tickets to get back to Africa. . . .

They raced off into the night.

"What *is* this place?"

"Eliza! I knew you'd save me!"

Eliza realized the horrible truth:

The **Blackburns** were the **poachers!**

"Go, Tally! That's it!"

"Tell me, or she goes over the edge!"

"Stop! I know because . . .

I can talk to animals!"

In a flash Eliza's powers were gone.

Debbie knew if anyone could save the elephants, Eliza could!

"You have to turn around!" Eliza screamed. She whipped off her necklace and threw it as hard as she could toward the fence. The elephants understood and stopped in their tracks!

Eliza got her powers back—on one condition: **"If you ever tell,"** Eliza warned Debbie, **"you'll turn into a baboon!"**

"They shot me"—The huge animal choked out the words—"at the river. . . . They were trying to take my horn when I ran away. . . ." And then he closed his eyes.

What should I do? Eliza wondered desperately. She looked more closely at his wound and gasped.

There was a knife tangled in the net that was stuck on the rhino's horn. Eliza grabbed the handle and pulled. But she couldn't pull it out!

Just then a van pulled up, and a man and a woman jumped out. They were dressed in dusty khakis. The woman carried a doctor's bag.

What luck! Eliza thought. "Please help me!" she cried. "This knife is stuck!"

Rushing over, the woman opened her bag. "Sloan, quickly!" she called to the man.

"Coming, Bree." Sloan Blackburn wrapped two hands around the knife and slowly pulled it free. The woman pressed bandages to the gunshot wound to stop the bleeding.

"Hold this," she instructed Eliza.

Eliza was glad to help. She watched the woman use her stethoscope to listen to the rhino's heart. "Is he still alive?" Eliza asked.

Bree's brow wrinkled in concern. "Barely, but I think I can save him."

Eliza watched as the woman carefully examined

the suffering rhino. What a wonderful career, to help wounded animals. Maybe that's something I could do when I grow up, she thought. I could do something other vets can't—ask the animal what's wrong!

"You're a brave young lady," Sloan said, wiping the blood from the knife with a handkerchief. "We saw you jump from that train."

"I had to save this rhino, I—"

Eliza froze as she stared at the knife in horror. The handle was unusual. She'd seen it before.

"That's the knife from the man who took Tally!" she cried.

Sloan stared at her in confusion. "Excuse me?"

"Keep applying pressure!" Bree ordered.

"I'm sorry," Eliza said, pressing again against the rhino's wound. "I just—"

But the sound of an approaching jeep made Sloan turn. "Thank goodness," he said. "The authorities."

A park ranger jeep drove up beside them. Three rangers climbed out and came over to examine the rhino.

"I'm Tim," a young ranger said, introducing himself. "What happened here?"

"Poachers shot him and then tried to take his horn," Eliza said, pointing to the knife Bree held. "They're at the river. Please, you must find them! They took a cheetah cub, too!"

Tim looked confused. "A cheetah?"

"I recognize their knife," Eliza explained. "Please, call Jomo Mbeli—"

"You know Jomo?" Tim asked, surprised.

"Yes, he's a family friend," Eliza answered, growing impatient with all the questions. "You have to go right now! They might be getting away!"

Tim looked at Sloan and Bree. "You are her parents?"

Sloan shook his head. "No, we just got here ourselves." He turned to Eliza. "We were just at the river," he told her. "There was no sign of poachers." He reached out to shake the ranger's hand. "I'm Sloan Blackburn, by the way. We're studying the endangered wildlife."

Bree stood up. "And there will be one less rhino if I don't get this poor creature to our camp."

"My wife, Bree," Sloan introduced her. "She's a wildlife veterinarian."

Tim shook hands with them, then gestured at the rhino. "Thanks but we'll take him to the rhino sanctuary." He shouted a command in a language Eliza recognized as Masai. His men came forward and slipped a carrier beneath the wounded rhino and began loading him into the jeep.

"But what about the poachers?" Eliza exclaimed. "They've got a cheetah cub!"

"You say you saw this knife before?" Tim asked.

"Yes." Eliza covered her face with her hands, remembering the man with the knife, remembering her fall from the helicopter's rope ladder. Remembering Tally's cries and Akela's face. "I'll never forget it."

Sloan examined the knife as he turned it over in his hand. "Figures it would belong to a poacher." He held it out for them all to see. "See this handle? It's made of ivory."

"Oh, no!" Eliza groaned, suddenly realizing her mistake. "I messed up the fingerprints when I touched it."

"It is not much use to us now," Tim admitted. "But I will call Jomo. And who are you again?"

"Eliza. Nigel Thornberry's daughter. He'll know."

Tim nodded and moved toward the jeep.

Bree smiled in surprise. "Nigel Thornberry? We watch his show all the time. Don't we, Sloan?"

"Wouldn't miss it," Sloan agreed. "Eliza, can we give you a lift somewhere?"

"Uh, no, thanks," Eliza said. "Our camp's not far from here."

"Send a truck to the river!" Tim called to his men. "Just to make sure!"

"Well, we do have to get back to our work." Bree smiled at Eliza. "But I hope we see you again."

"Me too. Thanks." Eliza watched them drive

away. She hoped she would see Bree Blackburn again. She wanted to ask her more about her work with animals.

Eliza turned back to Darwin. "Come on! We have to find those poachers!"

Darwin folded his arms and shook his head. "Uh-uh. No, we don't," he said stubbornly.

"But, Darwin, you saw what they did to that rhino!"

Darwin shuddered. "That's why we're going straight to your parents!" he insisted.

Eliza sighed. "You're right. My dad will know what to do." She took Darwin's hand, and they began walking alongside the train track.

"It's not far, is it?" Darwin asked.

"We'll get there by morning."

Darwin groaned as they walked off into the setting sun. "Oh, I wish we never left Lady Beatrice's. Thunder said there'd be days like this."

▪   ▪   ▪

The Thornberrys Commvee was parked alongside a river.

"We'll be gone until after the eclipse," Nigel told Debbie. "Will you be all right alone with Donnie?"

Debbie glanced at the picnic table. Donnie was doing his wedgie dance with three baboons, who imitated his every move. "Are you kidding?" she said flatly. "This will be the highlight of my young life."

Nigel grinned broadly. "That's the spirit, poodles!"

Debbie stared at her father. "Dad, have you completely lost your ability to recognize sarcasm?"

"I'm not sure I ever had it, Deborah," Nigel admitted. "Now, stay close to camp. If you're lucky, you might see a hyena roving about."

Debbie rolled her eyes. "Excuse me while I go find a container for my joy."

"Very well," Nigel said. "We'll wait right here—" He stopped, thought, and nodded. "Oh. That's sarcasm, isn't it?" Then his face fell. "Oh. You do that rather frequently, don't you?"

Marianne shook her head in exasperation. "Debbie, just how long is this sulking going to go on?"

Debbie glanced at her watch. "Another thirty-five, forty minutes. Then I'll start up again tomorrow."

"Well, get some rest," Marianne said, employing a little sarcasm herself, "I know it must be draining." She picked up her equipment, and she and Nigel headed off into the forest. "Be careful—and have a good time!"

"No problem," Debbie muttered. "I'll take the Congo-Com for a spin."

"Absolutely not!" Marianne called back over her shoulder.

Whoa. Like, my parents have bat ears, Debbie thought.

"But do have fun!" Nigel called cheerfully.

"And remember to watch Donnie!" Marianne added before they disappeared beyond the trees.

Donnie was still doing his wedgie dance. Then one of the baboons jumped in front of Debbie and wiggled his bare purple backside the same way.

Debbie flinched. "That is *so* wrong."

The evening went downhill from that point on. Debbie sulked, imagining what fun Eliza must be having in London.

But at last it was Donnie's bedtime. All she had to do was read him a couple of fairy tales, and she'd have the rest of the evening to herself to mope about how miserable she was.

She made Donnie change into his pj's, then tucked him into bed.

She held a big picture book of fairy tales up for him to look at. "So this cute dude named Jack plants these magic beans 'cause he's, like, hungry," Debbie began. "Then a mondo beanstalk grows overnight, way up into the clouds. . . ."

As Debbie read, she heard some small thumps on the roof. She glanced out the window. Bush babies.

71

How annoying, she thought. "So, Jack, who's totally buff by the way, climbs the beanstalk and he finds a golden goose, a golden harp, and a big scary—"

THUMP!

Something landed *hard* on the roof. The Commvee trembled.

"Giant?" Debbie squeaked. "Okay, that was definitely too large to be a bush baby."

Donnie bolted out of bed and into the tiny kitchen, where he crawled into one of the cupboards. Debbie crept after him. "Donnie!" she whispered.

Another *thump* sounded—right above her head!

Debbie screamed.

Donnie leaped out of the cupboard wearing a suit of armor made of pots and pans. He brandished a wooden spoon like a sword and charged out into the night.

Debbie grabbed the flashlight her parents kept by the door and cautiously crept down the steps.

Once outside she pointed the flashlight toward the sky.

"What in the world?" Debbie said, as she saw a large brown leather suitcase dangling from a parachute. It landed with a loud *thump* next to two other suitcases on the roof of the Commvee. Then she heard:

"Radcliffe! You never told me how to land!"

Strapped into a parachute, Cordelia Thornberry was hurtling toward the ground.

"Grandmumsy?!" Debbie exclaimed.

"It's all in the knees, Cordy!" a man's voice said.

Debbie spotted her grandfather, Colonel Radcliffe Thornberry, dangling from a tree in which his parachute had caught.

"Colonel?!"

"You're looking well, Deborah," her grandfather said nonchalantly, as if they had all just sat down to tea. "Do we have a kiss for Grandpapa?"

Debbie ran to the tree to help him just as Cordelia landed on the ground, instantly trapped beneath her huge white parachute.

Donnie raised his wooden spoon and began to strike at the squirming lump.

"Will *somebody* get me out of here?!" Cordelia's muffled voice cried.

"'Somebody'?" Debbie asked. "We'll talk about your impertinence later, Grandmumsy."

As she and Donnie helped Cordelia out from beneath the parachute, the last suitcase landed on the ground.

CRASH!

Cordelia peeked out from beneath the edge of the parachute. "I knew I shouldn't have brought the good china."

．．．

A short time later Cordelia placed several cups of steaming hot tea on the table inside the Commvee's tiny kitchen.

Then she announced, "Dreadful news, Debbie. Your sister has run away from Lady Beatrice's."

"Under the cover of night," the Colonel added. "With Darwin."

"Excuse me?" Debbie stared. "Did you say the *monkey* got to go to London?!"

The crackle of the shortwave radio interrupted them. "Debbie, are you there? Over."

Debbie leaped toward the radio and snatched up the mike. "Mom! Guess who's here!"

Before she could say another word, Cordelia seized the microphone and covered it with her hand. "There's no need to alarm your parents," she said firmly.

"What your grandmother means," the Colonel added, "is there's no need to have Marianne blame her a minute earlier than necessary."

Cordelia shot the Colonel a look, then told Debbie, "Eliza was seen boarding a train heading to the Congo. We'll take her back to London the minute she arrives."

Debbie twirled a lock of her hair and thought.

"Debbie?" Marianne's worried voice crackled over the shortwave. "Who's there?"

Cordelia gave Debbie a meaningful look and handed her the mike.

"Uh, just some cute bush babies," Debbie finally said.

"Debbie?" Marianne sounded shocked. "Did I just hear you call a wild animal cute?"

"That's called 'sarcasm,' dearest," Nigel said in the background.

Chapter 7

It was hot and dusty. And Darwin hadn't had any Cheese Munchies for days.

He and Eliza had walked most of the night. And now they were hitching a ride on a chicken cart pulled by a zebu.

Darwin pouted. How humiliating! he thought. Eliza and the zebu had chatted like long-lost pals. She had explained to Darwin that a zebu was a domesticated oxen—a work animal commonly used in these hot regions because it was a breed particularly resistant to heat and insect attack.

Swat!

"So that's why all the insects are biting *me!*" Darwin said miserably. "How did I end up here, amongst chickens?" he moaned. "Me, a once-proud honor student of Lady Beatrice's . . ."

A chicken poked her beak out of one of the cages. "Hey, who's the freeloader?" said the chicken. "At least we had seats on this cart!"

"Of course you have 'seats,'" Darwin retorted. "You're the guests of honor . . . at *dinner!*"

"Darwin!" Eliza scolded. Then she smiled at the chickens. "Don't worry," she assured them. "You're laying hens. I asked."

"Nice save," Darwin whispered in her ear. "Speaking of dinner, I'm starving."

Eliza pulled a wrapped sandwich from her backpack. "Here. It's the only thing they had left at the snack bar on the train."

Darwin eyed the sandwich. He sniffed at the wrapping and wrinkled his nose. "With good reason. Do you smell this? Ugh! Stinkbug on rye!"

Then he noticed the chickens staring at his food. "Don't get any ideas," he warned. "I may become desperate enough to eat this."

As the cart jolted along the bumpy road the driver of the cart sang a travel song in Swahili. Darwin sank against Eliza.

"How will you plan to explain all this to your parents?" he asked Eliza.

"I'm sure they'll understand," she said, "after I tell them about my dream."

Darwin rolled his eyes. "Oh, yes. It's perfectly reasonable," he said sarcastically. "You tell them you saw Tally, then you saw the Shaman, who told you that you must go back, and they'll say, 'Who?' and you'll say, 'Oh, the man who gave me the power to talk to animals,' and they'll say, 'What?' and you'll say, 'Oh, that's right, you don't know I can talk to animals!!'"

"Will you just eat the stinkbug sandwich already?" one of the chickens squawked.

Darwin scowled and hunkered down over his sandwich. "It isn't *literally* stinkbug on rye, you peabrain," he said as he peeled back the wrapper. "That's a metaphor—Agh! Look! They left the crusts on!" he complained. "Those animals!"

•   •   •

Back at the Thornberry camp, Debbie was up early trying to set up her parents' shark cage. This will work great as a cage . . . er, *playpen* for the wild boy, she thought. Her grandparents were still sleeping, so if she could just get Donnie contained, she could do something important. Like paint her nails.

"Donnie, this may *look* like a shark cage," she explained, "but it's really a playpen. It's where nice little boys play when their sisters want peace and quiet."

At last! The final piece snapped into place. She pulled a padlock and key from her pocket and went to lock the door.

Suddenly Donnie's eyes lit up and he shot out of the cage right through Debbie's legs . . .

And right into the arms of Eliza.

"Hey, Donnie!" Eliza exclaimed, tousling his hair.

"Well," Debbie said frostily, "if it isn't the boarding school dropout and her sidekick, Chimp-O."

"Save it, Debbie. I need to talk to Mom and Dad."

"Well, they're not here. You can talk to me and pretend I'm listening."

"Where are they?"

"Off in the jungle, filming some solar thing."

"But the eclipse isn't until tomorrow!" Eliza exclaimed.

Debbie picked at some chipped purple nail polish on her thumb. "Whatever."

"Fine." Eliza stomped toward the Commvee. "I'll call them on the radio."

"Uh, uh, uh." Debbie folded her arms. "I wouldn't go in there if I were you."

"And why not?" Eliza peeked inside. She gasped when she saw her grandparents, then quietly closed the door and tiptoed down the steps. "What are *they* doing here?"

"Taking you back to England," Debbie said, then frowned. "Not that you *deserve* to go."

"Well, I'm not going back!" Eliza insisted. "I'm

going to Tembo Valley where Mom and Dad are filming the eclipse. I need their help."

Debbie thrust her hands on her hips and stared at her sister. "What is *wrong* with you?" she exclaimed. "You finally get a chance to escape our mobile jail, and instead you come back like some freaky homing pigeon. I don't know about you, but I'm not gonna slow-dance at my prom with some purple-butt baboon!"

Eliza ignored her sister. She didn't have time to argue with Debbie today. She had a friend to save.

She strode to the picnic table and began to stuff bottled water, a compass, and other supplies into her backpack.

Eliza slung the backpack over her shoulder and started to leave. But Debbie blocked her way.

"Hey! I'm talking to you!" Debbie shouted.

"Debbie, leave me alone," Eliza said, trying to shove past. "I have something important to do, and you're not going to stop me!"

"Oh yes, I am! If I let you go, I get in trouble." She grabbed Eliza by the arm.

"Debbie—no!" Eliza wheeled around, desperately trying to break free and accidentally flinging her sister into the shark cage.

Shrieking in protest, Debbie tumbled to the ground.

Donnie scampered over and clicked the padlock shut, then ran off with the key.

Debbie scrambled to her feet and shook the bars. "Hey! Let me out of here!"

But Eliza couldn't let Debbie turn her over to her grandparents. They would take her back to England, and then she'd never save Tally!

"Sorry, Deb. You'll have to take it up with the warden. Come on, Darwin!"

Darwin dropped a stick covered with termites he'd been snacking on and ran after Eliza. No way did he want to be here when Debbie got free from that cage!

Debbie glowered as she watched Eliza and Darwin disappear into the forest. Just wait till I get my hands on that traitor—after everything I've done for her! Debbie thought ruefully.

"Donnie!" she called in her sweetest voice. "Bring me the key like a nice little animal-boy. . . ."

Donnie stopped and stared at the key in his hand. He stared at Debbie. With a shriek, he threw the key onto the ground and scampered after Eliza and Darwin.

Debbie shook the cage in frustration. "Grandmumsy! Colonel!" she hollered.

Her grandparents slept through it all.

Furious, Debbie dropped to the ground and

reached through the bars. She couldn't reach the key. But she could reach—*Ewwww!*—Darwin's termite stick, teeming with bugs—and Darwin's slobber. Debbie could barely stand to touch it, but she was able to use the stick to flick the key within reach.

Within minutes Debbie unlocked the cage, scribbled a quick note to her grandparents, and jumped onto the Congo-Com. "Yes!" she shouted in triumph as she roared off into the jungle. "Look out, Eliza Thornberry!"

Debbie tore through the jungle as if she were on her way to a Des Brodean concert. She dodged branches, vines, and other creepy stuff, feeling totally cool, even though she knew she was probably ruining her just-shampooed hair.

She hit a bump and flew into the air, then slammed back down in her seat. She pulled the Congo-Com to a stop.

"When I get my hands on that ungrateful, trouble-making know-it-all sister, I am going to—"

But then it hit her. Thanks to her dopey sister, she was cruising in the coolest vehicle around, without any parents to tell her how to drive. "Whoa! If I weren't so mad, this would totally rock!" Debbie said to herself.

Debbie revved the motor and raced out onto a log bridge. . . .

Only it wasn't a bridge. The log didn't go all the way across.

This is *so* not cool, Debbie thought as she plunged down a ravine. She managed to land upright on the ground below.

"I am driving around this sweaty jungle looking for my ungrateful sister when I could be sitting in front of the AC watching Part II of *Before They Were Teens*. And on top of that, I am probably getting helmet head!"

Debbie tore off the hot helmet and pulled a small comb from her pocket. Bending over at the waist, she flipped her hair over her head and began to brush the crimps out.

Behind her, a half-dozen forest elephants quietly lumbered by on their thickly padded feet.

Debbie missed it all.

Chapter 8

"*Both* of my daughters are missing?!" Marianne exclaimed when she heard the news.

She clutched Nigel's hand as they perched high in a tree, tied into harnesses, where they'd been watching for elephants.

Cordelia had just called them over the shortwave radio to tell them the news.

"But the good news is, the chimpanzee turned up—in England," Cordelia continued, trying to sound upbeat. "But never mind that now. Debbie left a note. 'Don't freak'—That's Deborah talking, not I—'Took the Congo-Com to find Donnie, who followed Eliza and Darwin to some valley. Later, Debbie.'"

Marianne gasped. "My children are in the jungle? *Alone?!*"

Nigel patted his wife's shoulder. "We'll find them, lovely." Then he spoke into the radio: "I say, Dad, are you there?"

"Right here, my boy."

"You'll have to pick us up downriver," Nigel told him. "I'll give your our coordinates. Can you triangulate a position?"

"They don't call me Colonel for my chicken recipe!" the Colonel quipped. "Fire away!"

• • •

Eliza and Darwin trudged through the dense, humid jungle. Their faces dripped with sweat. Bees dive-bombed their heads, and bugs crawled up their legs. The random shrieks of parrots made their hearts lurch.

"Oh, it's all coming back to me," Darwin moaned. "The unbearable humidity, the annoying bugs, the disappearing Donnie . . ."

Donnie had caught up with them, but then he ran off and got lost again.

"How am I supposed to look for my parents, the poachers, Tally, *and* Donnie?" Eliza said in frustration. She swatted a mosquito at her neck and felt her father's medal. His medal for bravery, she remembered. "Donnie!" she shouted into the jungle. *"Donnnnieeee!"*

"Donnie, this is no time for games!" Darwin shouted crossly. *"Eeeek!"* He came face-to-face with a five-hundred-pound gorilla crashing through the brush.

"Sorry!" Darwin squeaked as he ducked behind Eliza. "I didn't mean you!"

With a weary sigh, the gorilla held up a jabbering Donnie by the seat of his pants. "Does this . . . uh, little human belong to anyone?"

Eliza reached for Donnie. "Thanks. I hope he wasn't any trouble."

"Not really," the gorilla replied politely. "But you might want to tell him that when a gorilla is sleeping, he doesn't want a dung beetle shoved up his nose."

Donnie held one nostril and blew a bug out the other.

Eliza winced. "We're hoping it's just a phase." Then she added, "I'm looking for my parents. Have you seen two people on the way to Tembo Valley?"

The gorilla looked alarmed. "Were they riding in those loud whirly-birds?"

"No, they . . . *wait!* Do you mean helicopters?" She turned to Darwin, who was still trembling behind her, and said, "It could be the poachers!"

She turned back to the gorilla. "Did you see them? Did they have a cheetah cub with them? His name is Tally and—"

"Slow down," the gorilla said, holding up his humanlike hands. Then his voice hardened and anger flashed in his eyes. "I know about poachers. If these people are what you say, none of us is safe. I saw them building a fence across the valley."

"A fence?" Eliza exclaimed, puzzled.

Darwin tugged on her arm. "Now, Eliza, people build fences all the time. To keep animals in, to keep them out . . ."

"But there's no reason here," Eliza objected. "All the animals stay in the forest." She shook her head. "Something's up. What's the quickest way to the valley?" she asked the gorilla.

He pointed to a path behind her. "You can take a shortcut. Follow the river. But be careful—"

Eliza was already running toward the river. "Thanks!" she called out over her shoulder. "Dar, get Donnie!"

Darwin looked around. Where is that trouble-some boy? he wondered.

Suddenly Donnie jumped on Darwin's shoulders and shoved a beetle up the chimp's nose.

Gasping for breath, Darwin snorted and honked, trying to get it out.

"Don't force it, chimp," the gorilla advised from experience. "It'll come out in its own good time." As if to prove his point, the gorilla sneezed, and a bug flew out of his nose. He handed it to Donnie, who cooed with delight.

Darwin rolled his eyes. He missed London—and civilization—more and more with every passing second.

- - -

Marianne dreaded nightfall. She still had not laid eyes on her children. Where were they? Were they all right? Oh, why did they ever send Eliza away!

Marianne and Nigel were riding on the roof of the Commvee as it chugged down the Congo River. They drank strong black coffee with Cordelia and the Colonel to stay awake as they continued to search for the children.

"So you see, as many as one thousand elephants will converge during the eclipse," Nigel was saying, his voice wracked with guilt. "I am afraid my desire to witness a natural wonder might have influenced Eliza. She must have decided she couldn't miss it."

But Marianne shook her head. "No. Eliza wouldn't come all the way from London just for that. There's something else going on—" Her voice choked in a sob. "I'm just afraid that she'll get hurt."

"She'll be fine, Marianne," the Colonel said confidently. "They all will."

"Well, how do you know, Colonel?" Marianne asked tearfully. "And don't say, 'Because they're Thornberrys.'"

The Colonel reached for her hand. "No," he said, his voice gentle. "Because they've been raised by you. And quite wonderfully, I might add."

Surprised, Marianne smiled through her sniffles.

"Radcliffe is right," Cordelia said kindly. "Now let's find them!"

•   •   •

Debbie had survived the plunge down the ravine. She'd survived bugs and dirt and grime. She'd even survived helmet head and the heat and humidity that gave her a bad case of the frizzies.

But now as she drove slowly through the gathering darkness, she wondered if she could survive a night alone in the forest. Night sounds that seemed harmless when her parents and Eliza were with her now seemed scary enough to peel the polish off her toenails.

"Eliza! Donnie!" she shouted. "I have had enough of this! I am *not* in the mood!" Then she buried her face in her hands as she realized: "Oh, great. I'm turning into Mom!"

A large bird flapped across her path, its hoot echoing eerily through the forest.

"Where are the lights on this thing?" she grumbled nervously, pounding the control panel on the Congo-Com, looking for headlights.

The lights flicked on, spotlighting a startled antelope in her path.

Debbie shrieked and wrenched the steering wheel to the right, which landed her deep in a pool of mud. As she struggled to get the Congo-Com to go, she fell into the mud. "HELP!" she screamed as she began to sink into the strange quicksandlike goo.

Her scream attracted two wild boars, who crashed out of the forest and ran toward her with menacing grunts.

"Ahhh! Get out of here, pork chops!"

Suddenly something dropped down from above her head and scared the boars away.

Debbie looked up into the face of a native teenage boy, who was leaning down from a thick tree branch. His strong hands grasped hers and pulled her from the quicksand.

As he lowered her to solid ground, she brushed herself off, suddenly self-conscious. Sweaty and covered in mud was not the best way to meet a new guy.

She smiled at him as he slid down the tree. Then realized he was barely five feet tall.

"Uh, hi. Thanks," she said. "Oh, I don't normally look this bad. Just so you know. Which reminds me . . . have you seen a dorky girl with braces, a monkey wearing clothes, and a wild boy?"

The boy spoke rapidly in his own language and shrugged, shaking his head.

"I know. I don't get it either," Debbie said, not realizing that he couldn't understand English. "You have no idea what kind of day I've been having. Do you have a sister?"

The boy shook his head again, then pointed to himself. "Boko," he said.

"Oh, sorry, that was rude. I'm Debbie. Hey, Boko, you don't have a premoistened towelette on you by chance, do you?"

Debbie suddenly had the strange feeling that someone was watching her. Someone besides Boko. As she looked around, men, women, and children seemed to appear like magic from the trees around her.

They spoke to Boko in his native language. They pointed at the mud, at the Congo-Com, at Debbie.

Boko spoke rapidly, pointing to Debbie. Obviously explaining what had happened.

"Oh. No one speaks English?" Debbie finally realized.

The people surrounded her, smiling, nodding, gesturing for her to follow them.

With one last glance at the Congo-Com, Debbie let them lead her into the forest as she nervously looked around at the growing darkness.

"I am *so* grounded."

Chapter 9

A light! Could it be? . . .

Eliza ran toward it. In the distance, through the trees, she could see a campfire!

"Darwin! There's my parents' camp!" She and Darwin sprinted toward the light, with Donnie following at a distance.

"Mom! Dad!" she cried.

But as she ran into the clearing, she skidded to a stop. The two people eating supper around the campfire weren't her parents. But she knew who they were.

Sloan and Bree Blackburn!

"Eliza!" Bree exclaimed, clearly shocked to see the young girl alone in the dark. "What are you doing out here?"

But before Eliza could answer, Donnie stormed into the clearing behind her, screeching like a wild animal.

Bree reeled backward. "What's that?"

"It's okay," Eliza assured her. "It's just Donnie." Then she added, "Boy, am I glad to see you guys. Can I use your radio?"

"Of course," Sloan said. "But what's this all about?" He pointed to a large rock near the campfire. "Sit down. You look exhausted."

"I can't stay," Eliza protested. "I have to get to the Tembo Valley. The poachers are there, putting up some kind of fence. I just know something awful is going to happen!"

Sloan's face contorted in the flickering light of the fire. "How do you know? Did you see them?"

"I just—"

Oops. Eliza caught herself just in time. She knew the Blackburns loved animals as much as she did. But she couldn't reveal to them how she learned about the poachers' plans. I can't tell them I heard about it from a gorilla who saw it with his own eyes, she thought. "I have to find my parents," she said instead. "They went there to film the elephants."

"That's why we're here too!" Bree exclaimed with a smile. "To count the elephant population. If we can find any, of course."

"Yeah, they're really hard to find, they—" Eliza's hands flew to her face as she suddenly realized what the poachers were planning. "Oh, no!" she moaned.

Sloan looked worried. "What's wrong?"

Eliza sank in despair as she remembered what her father had told her about the elephants the night before she left for England. "They stay in the forest . . . except during the eclipse. . . . The poachers must have heard the legend." She looked up at the Blackburns, her eyes wide with fear. "They're after the elephants!"

"What?" Sloan gasped.

"No!" Bree cried in disbelief.

The Blackburns looked as horrified as Eliza felt.

"There's going to be thousands of them," Eliza cried, "out in the open! We have to call Jomo!"

Sloan strode toward a table set up outside their van. He tinkered with the radio, then turned, a look of frustration on his face. "No signal. Of all times!"

"What?!" Eliza exclaimed, joining him at the table. "Can't you fix it?"

Bree came over and put an arm around them both. "Guys, let's stay calm," she said in a firm but soothing voice. "We can't do anything about it tonight. Tomorrow we'll find Eliza's parents and use their radio." She smiled kindly at Eliza. "It's settled."

Then she headed for the van. Babbling with curiosity, Donnie scampered after her. But Bree shut the door in his face.

"Bree's right, Eliza," Sloan said. "The poachers

won't try to go after the elephants before the eclipse."

"But I'm worried about Tally," Eliza protested, and at Sloan's puzzled look, she added, "The cheetah I told you about."

Sloan nodded sympathetically, but still insisted she stay. "Eliza, it's dark. No sense getting yourself lost in the jungle."

"I won't get lost."

Bree came out of the van carrying several sleeping bags. "Honey, it's not like the savanna. You can't ask for directions. . . ."

"That's what she thinks," Darwin whispered in Eliza's ear.

"Darwin, shh!" she whispered back.

"Here," Bree went on, "for you and your chimp and your brother—" She turned toward Donnie and spotted him creeping toward the van.

She shot a stern look at Sloan, who dashed over and grabbed the small boy. "No, no, Donnie!" he said with a forced chuckle. "Wouldn't want you to go in there and make a mess."

Bree spread the sleeping bags around the campfire. "You can sleep here. Are you hungry? I make a mean vegetarian chili," she added with a grin.

Eliza stared off into the darkness. How can I just sit here when Tally is in danger? When the safety of all those innocent elephants is at risk? Eliza thought. But maybe Bree was right. I can't help them if I get lost or hurt.

She turned back to Bree and managed a small smile. "That would be great. Thanks."

Bree smiled and began to ladle a delicious-smelling stew from a pot that simmered over the campfire.

Darwin dashed to the front of the line to be served first, and Bree laughed as he turned up his bowl, gobbling his food as if he hadn't eaten for days.

As Eliza gratefully dug into her own bowl of stew, she studied her hosts. They were both so nice. And, like her parents, they were devoting their lives to the study and protection of animals. Eliza felt that their shared love for wild animals had made them instant friends.

I'm lucky to have found them, she thought.

•   •   •

Soon Eliza, Darwin, and Donnie were asleep around the dwindling fire as the moon rose in the night sky.

Eliza tossed in her sleep, her dreams filled with worry about Tally and the elephants.

Real sounds and dreams overlapped. In the

distance she heard noises . . . drumbeats . . . an elephant trumpet call . . . a thousand muffled footsteps along the riverbank . . . Darwin snoring . . . Tally, calling her name. . . .

Donnie couldn't sleep. He prowled the camp, poking his nose into everything.

Chattering softly, he sneaked up to the Blackburns' van and peeked in the window.

Something inside made him jump up and down.

With a hoot, he scampered to the door and turned the handle. . . .

Chapter 10

Debbie awoke the next morning with shafts of sunlight beating down on her face.

She groaned. Her bed felt scratchy and hard like packed dirt.

She turned over and opened one eye.

I'm sleeping in a doghouse, she thought hazily.

Suddenly she bolted upright and looked around. Okay, so it wasn't a doghouse, but it was not much bigger. Some kind of mud-and-palm hut. And she was sleeping on a straw mat on the ground.

Then she spotted a gourd filled with orchids beside her bed. A beautiful brightly colored cloth lay folded neatly beside that. Delighted, she unfurled the fabric across her lap. "I'd look so hot in this!"

Seconds later she crawled out of the hut, wearing the orchids in her hair and the cloth wrapped around her waist like a skirt.

Now she remembered everything. She'd been

rescued by that boy, Boko. She looked around at his village. The women and senior citizens busied themselves with chores. Most of the men seemed to be gone—off to work or hunting or something.

Smiling, Boko ran over and showed her a bowl full of something brown. Babbling in his native language, he poured fresh honey over it and held it up to her.

Debbie smiled. What an awesome way to start the day—even if I can't understand a word he's saying, she thought. "Thanks, I'm starving!" she said. Since he didn't offer any silverware, she figured it was okay to scoop the stuff into her mouth with her fingers. "Yum," she said with her mouth full. "What kind of cereal is this?"

Boko said something in his own language and pointed at a nearby termite mound where little kids were collecting termites on a stick. Then he smiled and motioned for Debbie to eat.

Debbie suddenly stopped chewing. *Termites? I'm eating termites?!* Slowly she managed to swallow the food. Then she wiped her mouth with the back of her hand and handed the bowl back. "Mmm, delicious!" she said through clenched teeth. She didn't want to insult him—he'd saved her life! But no way could she swallow any more of that!

Then a group of men came into the clearing,

proudly pushing the Congo-Com—and it was clean and shiny!

"Oh, thank you!" She ran to it, thrilled it was in one piece. Plus, she had something important stashed in the sidecar.

She dug around in it, pulled out a can, and popped the tab. "My soda!" She gulped a huge mouthful, swished, then spat out all traces of the termite oatmeal.

She noticed Boko staring at her. "Oh, um, sorry. Do you want some?" She held out the can.

Boko cautiously reached for the soda and took a tiny sip. He made a face, but politely swallowed, then burped loudly. The villagers laughed.

"De-luscious," he said, imitating Debbie's English word.

Debbie smiled, then peeked at her watch. "I am really late for the whole 'finding-my-sister' thing."

She noticed Boko admiring her watch. "Pretty cool, huh? And it's waterproof up to three feet." Then she had a great idea—a way to thank Boko for all his help. She tugged off her watch and held it up. "Hey, why don't you keep it?"

Boko spoke strange words that sounded like a question.

Debbie nodded and fastened the watch around his wrist.

"There. Oh, and thanks for the skirt." She pointed to the wrap skirt, then pointed to him. "You did give me this, right?"

He nodded.

"Boko give Debbie?" she tried. I'm totally getting into the whole international exchange thing going on here, she thought.

Boko cocked his head, pointed at his watch, and tried, "Debbie give Boko?"

Debbie pumped a fist in the air. "Yeah!" To herself, she muttered, "I am *so* good at this communication stuff."

But it was time to say good-bye. She fluffed her long curly hair, tugged on her helmet, and climbed on the Congo-Com.

Boko and the villagers began speaking all at once. Debbie couldn't understand the words, but they sounded worried.

"I'll be fine, really," she told them. "I know exactly where I'm going."

As the villagers stepped back, Debbie revved the motor, then waved. "Bye, everybody! Bye, Boko!"

"Bye!" the villagers repeated.

Watching her go, one of the tribal elders shook his head. "She won't be safe out there alone," he said in his native tongue.

A moment later Debbie roared through camp again, clearly lost.

"Hmm," said another elder. "*We* won't be safe with her out there alone."

Boko ran to catch her. "Debbie! No!"

Debbie was delighted to hear him speak English. And flattered that he wanted to hang out. Like, who wouldn't rather spend the day chilling with a cute guy your own age than with a twelve-year-old brace face who thought she was Dr. Dolittle or something?

But sometimes you just had to do the family thing. She pulled the Congo-Com to a stop and sighed. "Boko, listen, you can't come. It's not that I don't like you . . . and it's not the height thing. I just can't drag you into this family drama. . . ."

Boko stared past her. He looked so upset.

Like, who could blame him, Debbie thought. She didn't see the five-foot rhinoceros viper slithering along a tree branch directly over her head.

"Things may get ugly," she tried to explain. "I have to find my brat sister, and believe me, she's good at this jungle stuff—"

The snake sprang!

Instantly Boko grabbed Debbie and shoved her out of the way.

Debbie started to protest . . . but then she saw

the enormous snake as it landed near her feet.

She couldn't even scream. She watched in silent horror as Boko wrestled the snake on the ground, then flung the writhing creature into the forest.

Boko spoke rapidly to her in his own language. She got the feeling he was saying something like, "You are very fortunate. That one was poisonous."

She reached into the sidecar of the Congo-Com and tossed a helmet and goggles to Boko. "Think these will fit?"

• • •

Darwin was dreaming about tea and crumpets and the soft feather beds at Lady Beatrice's School for Girls. . . .

Then someone shook him awake.

"Darwin!" Eliza whispered urgently. "Donnie's gone!"

The sun was up, but Darwin wasn't. He pulled the sleeping bag up to his chin and turned over.

"Darwin!" Eliza shook him again. "We need to find Donnie. The eclipse is in a few hours!"

"Oh, all right," Darwin said, pouting.

Eliza rushed to the Blackburns' van and tapped on the door. She hated to wake them up, but this was urgent. "Bree! Sloan! Have you seen Donnie? He's—"

The door swung open, and Donnie stood just inside, babbling excitedly.

Oh, no. The Blackburns told him to keep out of the van. She hoped he hadn't messed anything up. She tried to pull him out, but Donnie scampered back inside, calling to her.

Worried—and curious—Eliza stepped through the doorway.

Holy cow! Eliza thought. The inside of the Blackburns' van was filled with high-tech equipment. On the wall she spotted a map and looked more closely. It was a map of Tembo Valley, where the elephants would gather.

Darwin tugged at her arm and pointed to a couple of monitors. One showed a video of several men throwing nets over some baby chimps. Another showed scenes of tigers, rhinos, and bears being captured, shot, or trapped.

"What *is* this place?" she wondered aloud, horrified at the images she saw.

"I don't know, but I don't like it," Darwin whined. "We've got Donnie, now let's go."

But Eliza couldn't leave. Something was terribly wrong here. Sloan and Bree were good, kind people who cared about animals. But these videos . . .

She cautiously stepped forward and tripped on something. She glanced down and frowned. She'd kicked over a small bowl. Milk sloshed onto her boot.

Then she heard something. A tiny muffled voice. "Help . . ."

Eliza threw open cupboards, searched the floor, trying to find whoever needed help.

The voice grew stronger. "Help . . . Eliza . . ."

Eliza's mouth fell open. "Tally!"

She yanked open another cupboard, and there he was, crouching back in the corner. Now he stumbled out, blinking in the sudden bright light.

"Oh, Tally!" Eliza cried as she scooped him up in her arms.

Tally licked her face, he was so happy to see her. "Eliza! I knew you'd save me!"

But suddenly Tally growled.

Eliza slowly turned around.

Sloan Blackburn stood in the doorway, his face an unreadable mask. "Hello, Eliza."

Bree stood right behind him, stone-faced.

Eliza was confused. "This cheetah cub," she said, stroking Tally's fur. "Where did you get him?"

Sloan shrugged. "I picked him up . . . on the savanna."

Eliza stared in disbelief. "You *bought* him?"

"Oh, no," Sloan said with a strange smile. An evil smile. "I picked him up. Right off the ground."

Eliza trembled as she put the pieces of the puzzle

together in her mind. The man who stole Tally, the man she chased up the rope ladder, the man whose face she couldn't see . . . "It was you!"

Sloan reached down for the ivory-handled dagger he had tucked into his high-topped black boot.

It's the dagger that the poacher used! Eliza thought. The same one I pulled from the net!

"Yes," Sloan admitted, "and by the way, thank you for returning my knife to me."

Eliza paled as she realized . . .

Sloan was the poacher!

But Bree's a veterinarian, Eliza thought. She loves animals, I know she does. Eliza looked past Sloan to the woman who had been so kind to her. The woman Eliza admired. Surely Bree doesn't know what Sloan has done. . . .

Bree came forward and plucked Tally from Eliza's arms. Glancing down, she noticed the bowl of spilled milk. "Oh, kitten," she scolded Tally, "you didn't drink all your milk."

She *does* care! Eliza thought in relief. But Bree's next words turned her blood to ice:

"How are you ever going to grow big enough to make me a fur coat?" Bree purred into the tiny cub's ear.

Eliza gasped and stepped back—thankful that Tally couldn't understand Bree's horrible words.

Donnie tried to escape between Sloan's legs, but Sloan grabbed him and held him aloft. "Oh, no, Donnie. It isn't polite to leave without saying good-bye to your hosts." He smiled at Eliza in fake concern. "I'm afraid you'll have to miss the solar eclipse. But," he added, pointing at the monitors, "you can catch it on the Poaching Channel."

Eliza stared at the images. Now she began to realize. Kidnapping Tally was not Sloan Blackburn's only crime. He was planning to hurt the elephants, too. "You want the elephants, so you built the fence—," Eliza started to say.

"The electric fence, of course," Sloan replied as if it were something to brag about. "Now here's a question for your famous father. How many volts does it take to kill a thousand elephants?"

Chapter 11

Eliza struggled against the ropes Sloan Blackburn was using to tie her hands. She couldn't bear to look at Bree.

Darwin and Donnie were already tied up, back to back. Darwin looked scared. Eliza tried to whisper to him in chimp: "Don't worry! It'll be okay."

But how could it be? Her hands were tied.

"Eliza, you're a little troublemaker," Sloan said as he tightened the knots. "First you show up on my cheetah hunt. Then you jump from a train to save my rhino."

"He's not your rhino!" Eliza cried.

Sloan shrugged. "Have it your way. And somehow you knew that poachers had shot him at the river. Yet you were on a train at the time."

"I guessed."

"Perhaps." Sloan studied her and frowned. "And now you arrive in the jungle, knowing about the fence. A fence which no one has witnessed being

108

built. So, my little troublemaker . . . who told you?"

Eliza swallowed. "No one."

"Are your parents working with that Jomo person?"

"They don't even know I'm here."

"Then who's your source of information?" Sloan demanded.

"There's no one."

Sloan's face turned red with anger. "You know too much for a little girl! I have too much invested in this operation to let anything get in my way!"

A bolt of fear shot up Eliza's spine.

"If you don't tell me who they are," Sloan said calmly, "you'll be sorry. *Very* sorry."

Suddenly Bree poked her head in the door. "Sloan! I hear something."

Sloan glared at Eliza, then hurried outside.

As soon as Sloan was gone, Darwin began to chatter. "What's going on? I don't like the way that man is looking at us," he said.

"Eliza, I saw them with firesticks that make a loud sound," Tally said.

"Explosives?! We've got to get out of here!" Eliza declared.

The cub ran over and began to chew on Eliza's ropes with his sharp little teeth.

"Go, Tally! That's it!" Eliza cheered.

"Yes, that's it, get the cheetah involved again," Darwin said, as he struggled against his ropes. "If we hadn't gone out looking for them that night, we wouldn't be in this mess!"

"Don't blame Tally," Eliza said quietly.

"I'm not," Darwin insisted, sounding nearly hysterical. "Tally didn't sneak out without permission. . . . Tally didn't run away from boarding school. . . . Tally didn't trust those awful people who clearly don't like animals."

Eliza sighed. "I thought they were like me. . . ."

"When are you going to see that no one's like you?" Darwin shouted. "What more do you need? The Shaman gave you a gift, use it!"

"Darwin, please!"

"You know what I think? You don't know what to do with your powers—"

"Darwin, for once in your life just BE QUIET!"

Darwin gasped, his feelings deeply hurt.

Just then Tally chewed through a rope, freeing Eliza's hands. She jumped to her feet and began to look for a way to escape.

Outside she heard the sound of a motor.

Then voices.

"Hi. Can we help you?" she heard Bree ask.

"Yeah," someone said. "I'm looking for my sister, Eliza Thornberry."

Eliza gasped.

Debbie!

Sloan grabbed Debbie roughly by the arm.

"Hey!" Debbie shouted. "What do you think you're doing—"

"Debbie!" Boko cried. He leaped out of the Congo-Com and onto Sloan's shoulders, piggyback style.

Eliza charged out of the van. "Let her go!" she shouted at Sloan.

"Eliza?" Debbie exclaimed in surprise.

But then Bree grabbed Eliza. She struggled against Bree's tight grip and shouted, "Let my sister go!"

"Certainly," Sloan said with an evil smile. "If you tell me who was your source of information. . . ."

"I told you," Eliza cried. "There's no one. I just guessed at all that stuff . . . the fence and the explosives and . . ."

"I never mentioned explosives!" Sloan shouted.

He squeezed Debbie so tightly she was gasping for air. "What's . . . he . . . talking . . . about?"

Eliza watched in horror as Sloan dragged Debbie to the edge of a steep cliff. "Tell me, or she goes over the edge!"

"Please . . . ," Eliza begged. "She doesn't know about any of this!"

"Who told you these things?!" Sloan shouted.

"I can't tell you!" Eliza yelled.

Sloan started to throw Debbie over the cliff.

Debbie screamed.

"STOP!" Eliza cried, nearly in tears. "It was the animals!"

Sloan froze. He held Debbie teetering on the edge of the cliff. And waited for Eliza to say more.

Eliza took a deep breath. There was no way out of it. The Shaman had warned her never to tell anyone about her gift. If she told, she'd lose her power to talk to animals.

But nothing was more important right now that saving her sister's life.

"I know," Eliza admitted, "because I can talk to animals."

Chapter 12

A deafening *boom!* split the skies. A flash of white light nearly blinded them all.

A supernatural wind rose and a swirling vortex of animal images spun around Eliza, lifting her into the air and knocking the others to the ground.

Debbie crawled on her stomach, grasping grass and twigs, till she reached a tree to hang on to.

Boko shouted something to Debbie in his native language, then disappeared in the tornadolike winds.

Sloan and Bree fought their way to their helicopter just as—

CRASH!

Their van tipped over in the wind, shattering its windows. Donnie's head poked out, then Darwin's.

"Darwin!" Eliza shouted over the noise of the wind. "Come on!"

Darwin chittered excitedly in response. Chimp talk!

Eliza's heart sank. She couldn't understand a single word.

•   •   •

There was no time to be sad. Eliza ran to help Donnie and Darwin out of the wrecked van. Then she shooed them toward Debbie. "Debbie, run!" she shouted at her sister. "Into the woods!"

Debbie grabbed Darwin and Donnie by the hand and ran toward the forest. But then she glanced back and saw that Eliza wasn't coming. "Where are you going?"

"I have to get Tally!" Eliza shouted. She rushed back to camp, calling the cub's name. At last she found him huddled beneath the overturned van, too scared to move. Eliza lunged for him and pulled him into her arms.

Eliza, Debbie, Darwin, Donnie, and Tally ran through the forest, dodging falling trees and flying debris as lightning split the sky. The river was overflowing its banks as they scrambled onto a log that swept them out into the roaring rapids.

Eliza thought the storm would never end. But at last the winds died. The flashing lights ended. Sunlight danced along the river as it turned smooth as glass. The silence was eerie.

While Donnie, Tally, and Darwin gathered at the

front of the log, Eliza and Debbie sat side by side, dangling their feet in the water.

Debbie gave her sister a sidelong glance from beneath the curtain of her long blond hair. "Do you expect me to believe that a couple of years ago you saved a warthog, but he was really a magic man who made it so you could talk to animals, but you had to keep it a secret or else there'd be some tornado thing and you would lose your powers?"

"Well, yeah," Eliza said.

"I knew it!" Debbie cried, smacking the log with her hand. "That's why you're always sneaking out all the time with Darwin!" She shook her head, then had a sudden thought. "Did you tell that mountain goat to butt me down the Alps?"

"No!" Eliza insisted. "I don't use my powers that way!"

"Okay, okay. What about the time that python crawled into my tent?"

"That was your fault for leaving the flap open," Eliza pointed out. She shrugged. "I barely even talk to snakes anyhow."

"Okay, okay." Debbie combed out her hair with her fingers, thinking. "What about those spider monkeys that stole my bra off the clothesline?"

Eliza cringed. "Okay, that. But it was Darwin's idea."

"I knew it!" Debbie cried. "Oh, I have a few things to say to that monkey. Tell him I don't appreciate it when he leaves pizza crusts under the seat cushions. Go ahead, tell him."

"Debbie, I can't. I broke the rule," Eliza said sadly. "I knew if I told anyone about my powers, I'd lose them."

Debbie stared at her sister in amazement. "Omigosh. You did that . . . for *me?*"

Eliza nodded, fighting back tears. "So I can't talk to Darwin anymore. And the last thing I ever said to him was really mean. Now I can't even tell him I'm sorry."

If Eliza didn't know better, she might have thought she saw a tear in Debbie's eye.

Suddenly Darwin chattered loudly.

Debbie looked toward the front of the log. "Eliza, I may not speak monkey, but I think he's trying to tell us about that waterfall! . . ."

Just ahead of them a log disappeared over the edge.

"Oh, no!" Eliza cried. "Hang on!"

Just as they reached the edge, their log jammed along the bank. Slipping and sliding they managed to scramble up the bank.

They found themselves moving along the edge of a cliff just as the sun cast a warm glow across the beautiful land below.

"We're here," Eliza said. "This must be Tembo Valley." Then she heard a familiar noise and looked up at the sky. "Oh, no!"

The Blackburns' helicopter roared into view.

"Come on!" Eliza told her sister. "We have to stop them!"

Together they ran along the cliffs. But suddenly the land seemed to disappear and they were falling, down, down—till they landed on a soft earthen floor.

"Ow!" Debbie said. "What happened?"

Eliza looked around. They'd fallen through some kind of hole into a cave. "I don't know, but we have to get out of here!"

Darwin stood up and reached for Eliza's hand to help pull her up. Debbie watched in amazement as he helped brush the dirt from her clothes. "Darwin looks out for you, doesn't he?"

"Yeah. He's my best friend," Eliza said.

Then they heard another sound—a slow pounding rumble—and Eliza rushed to the entrance of the cave. She gazed down into the valley. "The elephants!"

Hundreds of forest elephants, young and old, were trampling through the valley. Their large, graceful bodies moved nearly in unison. It was a beautiful sight.

Debbie whistled in awe. "That's a lotta elephants."

But Eliza was beside herself with worry. "They're heading toward an electric fence, and I can't even warn them!"

"But can't you, like . . . make elephant noises or something?" Debbie suggested.

"I can't talk to them, Debbie!" Eliza cried. "How can I help them? You don't understand. Shaman Mnyambo told me in a dream that there was a bigger problem . . . but I can't do anything about it now."

Eliza sank to the ground, fighting back tears. Hundreds of elephants were about to die. And it felt as if it were all her fault.

"Okay, enough with the 'poor me, I lost my magic powers' bit." Debbie gave her sister a nudge with her foot. "Are you just going to sit there?"

"What am I supposed to do?" Eliza said miserably. "I'm just an ordinary girl now."

"Yeah, right." Debbie rolled her eyes, then sat down beside her sister. "Ever since you were a little kid, you dragged home birds with broken wings, creepy toads, and other stuff. You didn't have special powers then," she pointed out. "You just cared. Trust me, you were never 'ordinary.'" Debbie shrugged, trying not to get too mushy. "It's like you were born for this or something."

Eliza smiled up at her sister, her eyes brimming with tears. It was the nicest thing Debbie had ever said to her. She reached for her hand and squeezed it.

Maybe there's nothing I can do to help the elephants, she thought. But Debbie's words made her feel as if she had to at least try.

Chapter 13

The Commvee raced along the river. Nigel and the Colonel searched the terrain through their binoculars.

"Do you see the girls?" Marianne asked anxiously. "Or Donnie?"

The Colonel shook his head. "No, but . . . Nigel, what do you make of that?"

Nigel adjusted the focus on his binoculars. He could see to the end of the valley. Electric cables were strung across the river. And nearby he saw men gathered around some sort of electric generator. "Poachers!" Nigel exclaimed. "They're setting up explosives."

He lowered his binoculars and looked at his wife. "The barbarians are going to frighten the elephants into an electrical fence. Marianne, step on it!"

Marianne hit the gas, and the Commvee leaped forward, speeding over the crevice through which their girls had fallen into the cave.

- - -

Unaware they'd just missed their parents, Eliza led the others out of the cave onto a narrow ledge of a cliff.

Below they could see the elephants parading peacefully toward the sun.

Eliza grabbed hold of a vine.

"Eliza, no!" Debbie cried.

But Eliza disappeared over the side of the cliff.

"It's not too late to become ordinary!" Debbie called after her.

Then she heard the sound of a motor coming from behind. Someone called to her. "Debbie!"

Debbie whirled around. "Boko!" He was in the driver's seat of the Congo-Com! She jumped in beside him.

Meanwhile, Eliza had landed safely on the ground. Seconds later a nervous Darwin slithered down the rope behind her, whining and fussing. Eliza wished she could understand what he was saying.

"Darwin, stay here," she told him, trying to make him understand through gestures. "I'll be back."

Darwin chattered frantically, but stayed put.

Eliza ran across the valley into the middle of the elephant herd. With no thought for her own safety, she pushed on their enormous legs, trying to make them understand. Trying to make them stop.

"Please, no!" she shouted. "Go back! Turn around!"

But the gentle creatures pressed forward, carefully stepping around her as she ran between them.

- - -

Hovering over the valley in his helicopter, Sloan Blackburn cursed when he spotted the Commvee barreling down into the valley.

"It's the kids' parents!" Furious, he shouted into his radio, "Set off the first round of explosives. *Now!*"

The men on the ground instantly obeyed his order.

At the sound of the explosions, the elephants panicked. They reared back and trumpeted, breaking into a stampede.

Down below, Nigel and Marianne cringed at the sounds.

"Marianne, try to get to the fence and short it out," Nigel suggested. "Dad and I will take care of the explosives. Ready, Dad?"

The Colonel saluted. "Let me at 'em, boy!"

The two men leaped out of the Commvee and ran toward Sloan's ground crew.

Cordelia snagged the radio mike and shouted, "Jomo? I say, are you there, Jomo?"

* * *

Nigel and the Colonel rappelled down the nearby cliff. With a few well-placed snips, they quickly clipped the wires connected to the explosives.

This time, when Sloan ordered his men to set off more explosives, nothing happened.

"They've been cut!" one of his men shouted through the radio.

* * *

Eliza struggled against the sea of elephants stampeding around her. "Stop!" she shouted. "Please!" As she ran alongside the herd, she caught the eye of the leader, a wise-looking old elephant. Something about her reminded Eliza of her friend Kianga. And that gave Eliza an idea.

She quickly ran ahead to a pile of rocks. As the elephant stomped by, Eliza leaped through the air . . .

And landed hard on the elephant's back. She scrambled to hang on. "Whoa! Okay . . . gotta stop her. . . ."

Eliza gently placed her feet along each side of the elephant's head. Then she nudged her behind the ear, just as she'd done with Kianga. "Please . . . you have to turn around . . . come on . . . ," she begged.

But the elephant kept walking, and all the other elephants followed her.

Eliza wouldn't give up. Finally the elephant trumpeted. Annoyed by this small girl on her back, she reached around with her trunk to shove her off. Eliza grasped the end of the trunk and rubbed it against the elephant's neck in the age-old sign of affection. "See?"

The elephant calmed down, but did not stop. The other elephants fanned out behind her as they kept going.

"This way. . . . Let's turn around now!" Eliza shouted. Oh, it was no use! Then she looked up ahead and what she saw sent chills down her spine.

They'd almost reached the fence!

"You have to turn around!" Eliza screamed. "It's an electric fence. . . . You'll all be killed! You have to stop!"

But some force seemed to pull the elephants forward, no matter what Eliza did. And then she realized . . .

The eclipse! Soon the moon would completely cover the sun.

Eliza fingered the necklace her father had given her, wishing she could absorb some of her father's quick thinking in a time of crisis. "I've got to think of something . . . quick!"

Then it came to her: The necklace! She only hoped her idea would work.

Chapter 14

It had to work!

Eliza whipped off the necklace and threw it as hard as she could toward the fence.

As the metal necklace fell, it bounced several times against the electric fence, setting off a shower of sparks.

The elephants reared back in fear.

"See? You have to turn! You can do this!" Eliza cried. "I know you can't understand me, but you have to trust me! Turn around!" She nudged the elephant she was riding again. And then something miraculous happened.

The elephant she was riding turned.

The other elephants stopped in confusion. But the lead elephant trumpeted a message.

Eliza didn't need the ability to speak elephant to know what she was saying. "I did it! You're telling them to stop!"

- - -

Sloan swooped down over the valley in his helicopter. "Olaf!" he shouted through his radio to one of his men on the ground. "They're turning around! Start shooting!"

Olaf looked through binoculars at the herd. He gasped when he spotted Eliza's red pigtails. "But there's a girl riding one of the elephants!"

"I don't care," Sloan barked. "Take down those elephants!"

"Forget it, Sloan. No way I'm hurting a kid!"

Sloan stared at his radio in disgust. "I'll take care of the kid." He turned to his wife, who was piloting the helicopter. "Bree, go low!"

Down below, the elephants continued to turn, heading away from the electric fence. "Keep going!" Eliza shouted gleefully. "That's right! We're almost out of here!"

But then Eliza heard the unmistakable sound of a helicopter roaring in over her head. She looked up.

Sloan Blackburn was hanging down from a rope ladder!

Eliza screamed as the poacher grabbed her by the arm and lifted her off the elephant's back. Then the chopper veered toward the river. Eliza dangled over the rapids.

Shaking with rage that this small girl had spoiled

all his plans, Sloan glared down at Eliza. "You will regret this!" he shouted.

"I don't care!" Eliza shouted back. "What you're doing is awful!"

"And what you're doing is *stupid,*" Sloan retorted. "Too bad you won't be here to help me carry all this ivory."

Only a man with a heart of stone could drop a twelve-year-old girl into a raging river.

Sloan let go.

Eliza screamed as she plunged into the churning waters below.

Chapter 15

"Sloan," Bree begged, "let's get out of here!"

"No!" Sloan shouted. "We're going back!"

Reluctantly she turned the chopper around. As they hovered over the elephant herd, Sloan aimed his gun.

But the elephants were angry. And Bree had flown too close. Several powerful bull elephants reached up with their mighty trunks, grabbed the helicopter, and yanked it down from the air. It crashed on its side, smashing and twisting its whirling blades.

Sloan and Bree tumbled onto the ground.

Dozens of elephants pinned Sloan to the ground. He was face to face with the elephants' sharp tusks.

As Bree scrambled to get away, Marianne drove up in the Commvee. "Cordelia," she ordered, "now!"

Cordelia dutifully pressed a button. A net flew from the Commvee's roof. It landed on Bree and she fell, tangled in its thick ropes.

• • •

Back at the river Debbie had arrived with Boko in the Congo-Com just in time to see Eliza fall. Now she ran frantically toward the riverbank, searching the water for her sister. "Eliza!" she shouted. *"Eliza!"*

Eliza's head bobbed to the surface, but then the currents pulled her back under.

Without a moment's hesitation, Debbie dove into the churning waters. As she fought the current, several hippos rose from the dark depths and surrounded her.

Boko shouted at Debbie, waving at her to come back to shore.

As he did, the moon's shadow moved across the sun, darkening the sky, with only a ring of light surrounding it like a halo. And then the moon moved past the sun, and the sky became bright again. Beneath it all, the river carried Eliza away.

• • •

Eliza struggled up from the depths of the river, her lungs bursting for air. An endless stream of images swam before her eyes: bubbles, fish, then sparkles of light, then—could it be true?—the face of Shaman Mnyambo.

As she fought her way to the surface she saw some kind of stick. She grabbed it, and a strong force pulled her up out of the water.

And then she saw him—the Shaman! It was really

him! The stick she saw was his staff.

With her last ounce of strength, Eliza climbed onto a rock in the middle of the river and clung to it, gasping for breath.

Then she remembered the elephants, and she began to cry. They must have all been killed by now, she thought.

"Shaman Mnyambo . . . I'm sorry," she said through her tears. "I messed everything up. . . . If I hadn't broken the rule, I could have saved them."

"But you did save them," the Shaman said. "Look."

Eliza straightened her glasses and looked toward the riverbank. The elephants! They were alive! It was the most beautiful sight Eliza had ever seen.

"And you did this not with your gift," the Shaman said, "but with your heart."

Eliza beamed at his praise.

The Shaman scratched his head with the end of his staff. "And if this is what you can do *without* your powers, you have a greater destiny than I've even known. So"—he said with a smile—"I'm going to grant you your powers back."

"You are?" Eliza gasped. "Really?"

The Shaman nodded. "But there's one small condition."

Eliza leaned in close.

"It's about your sister. . . ."

Chapter 16

Eliza said good-bye to the Shaman, then swam to shore. As she pulled herself out of the water onto the bank, a vehicle rolled to a stop in front of her.

"Need a lift?" called a familiar voice.

Eliza looked up. "Debbie!" she cried. She ran to the Congo-Com, and the two sisters hugged. Then Debbie introduced the native boy who sat in the sidecar beside her.

Boko smiled at Eliza and nodded in greeting. "Brat sister."

Debbie winced. "Uh, I don't know where he got that."

Eliza just laughed and climbed in. She knew she'd always be the little brat sister. But she and Debbie had almost lost each other today. And somehow she knew that things between them would never be quite the same again.

Suddenly Eliza spotted something up ahead—in the middle of all the elephants.

"Debbie, stop! There's Darwin!"

Debbie screeched to a halt, and Eliza jumped to the ground. She ran across the valley, weaving in between the elephants' legs, searching for one special animal.

And then she saw him. "Darwin?"

Darwin stomped toward her. "I know you think I talk too much, so from now on, I'm just going to sit back and quietly observe—"

"Yeah," Eliza said with a smile, "like that'll ever happen."

Darwin started to whine something back, then froze and his mouth fell open. "Eliza? Did you just *talk* to me?"

But for a moment Eliza couldn't talk. She just nodded as her eyes filled with tears.

Darwin squealed and threw his arms around her, laughing through his tears.

Eliza only broke free when she saw her parents. "Mom! Dad!"

"Poppet!" her father shouted.

"Oh, Eliza!" Marianne cried as Eliza ran into her arms. "Thank heaven, you're all right."

"My dear child," Cordelia announced as she, the Colonel, and Donnie gathered round, "I promise never to bring up boarding school again."

■　　■　　■

A short while later Boko gestured to Debbie that it was time for him to leave.

"So . . . you're going back to your family now?" she asked.

Boko looked sad and started to take off the watch.

"No! You keep it," Debbie insisted. "Friend?"

Boko smiled and nodded. "Friend."

Debbie waved good-bye to Boko as he headed back into the forest.

The Thornberrys gathered by the river as Marianne filmed the elephants. Watching all of the elephants bathing together was a magnificent sight.

"Wow," Eliza said to the lead elephant, whose name she now knew was Winna. "So that's why you all come here. . . ."

"Yes," Winna replied. "And thanks to you, my child, we will all leave here . . . safely." She affectionately stroked Eliza's neck with her trunk.

As Nigel joined her Eliza stared up at the sky. The remnants of the eclipse were barely visible.

"Pretty cool, huh, Dad?" Eliza said softly. "The legend was right."

"It was indeed, poppet. But I still wonder *why* they gather during an eclipse."

Eliza hesitated, then glanced at Winna. More than anything she wished she could tell her father. She knew how much it would mean to him to be able to talk to these animals.

But for now she would just have to do her best to share what she knew without risking the loss of her gift. "Maybe the elephants feel safe," she said.

"Safe?"

Eliza nodded. "Yeah. Maybe because it's the one day that everything changes . . . the little moon blocks the powerful sun. So maybe—"

"They have reason to hope," Nigel said, his eyes lighting up. "Maybe these intelligent creatures believe that by standing together, as they have done for centuries, they may, one day, live without fear of Man's greed." He smiled down at his youngest daughter. "What you did was extraordinarily brave, you know."

Eliza blushed. "Well, don't forget . . . my dad got a medal for that once."

Nigel chuckled.

Just then Winna splashed from the water and uncurled her trunk toward Eliza. She was holding something. Eliza reached for it and gasped. It was her father's medal!

Then Winna reared back her head and trumpeted a loud call.

"I don't know, of course," Nigel told his daughter, "but I'd swear she's thanking you."

Eliza blushed again. "I think so too, Dad," she said softly.

Then father and daughter watched the elephants in silence, for no words were needed to describe the feeling they shared.

- - -

A few days later, as the sun began to set on the Serengeti Plain, Eliza and Darwin once again walked through the tall grasses where they had played before the poachers interrupted all their lives.

Eliza was taking Tally back where he belonged. But where was his family?

Debbie was following them, frowning at Darwin's chimp chatter. "Ask him, Eliza. Did he or did he not take my hairbrush?"

Eliza chattered to Darwin in chimp, and Darwin answered defiantly.

Debbie stamped impatiently, frustrated that she couldn't understand. "Well?"

Eliza sighed. She was getting a little tired of Debbie following her around asking her to translate all the time now. "He says he was just *borrowing* it."

Darwin reluctantly pulled the hairbrush from the pocket of his blue shorts and held it out.

Debbie recoiled in disgust. "*Ewww!* Like I want it back with monkey fur on it!"

Eliza shrugged, and she and Darwin ran ahead.

Debbie shouted after them, "Okay, time to establish some ground rules! Tell Darwin that he is not to use any of my beauty products unless I have thrown them away. . . . Tell him . . ."

But Eliza was no longer listening. Her eyes widened in delight. Just ahead, in the shade of an acacia tree, Akela was bathing her cubs.

"Mom!" Tally cried.

Akela looked up in surprise. "Tally?"

Eliza set the cheetah cub on the ground, and he dashed toward his mother.

"Mom, Mom! I'm back! Eliza rescued me!"

"Tally! Oh, my baby!" Akela cried. "I never thought I'd see you again!"

Akela licked Tally all over to make sure he was all right as Cacia and Kosey ran over and began to wrestle and play with him.

Eliza and Darwin watched quietly, glad to be a part of the happy reunion.

Just then Debbie caught up with them. "Eliza, I was talking to you—"

But when she saw the happy cheetah family, even she was moved. "Wow. Cool," she whispered.

Then Akela leaped toward them.

Debbie froze in fear. "Hey, what's she doing? Tell her that's close enough."

Akela crept closer.

Debbie jumped behind Eliza, trembling. "Eliza! *Tell* her!"

Akela stopped in front of Eliza, and then purred a thank-you. Eliza smiled and purred back. The three cubs ran over and rubbed against her legs, and Eliza petted them.

Debbie stepped back, still scared in spite of her sister's friendship with the animals. "They don't bite, do they?"

Eliza whispered to the cubs, and they surrounded Debbie, rubbing up against her legs affectionately.

But then it was time to say good-bye. Akela called to her children, and they followed her off across the plains. Tally looked back at Eliza one last time, then disappeared in the tall waving grasses.

Eliza smiled with satisfaction. "Let's go home."

- - -

As they neared the Thornberry camp Eliza spotted her parents filming alongside a nearby watering hole, where a variety of animals and birds drank and bathed.

Marianne looked through her camera and shouted to Nigel, "You're on, honey!"

Nigel cleared his throat, then smiled into the camera. "Here at the watering hole, animals quench

their thirst in an atmosphere of peace and tran-
quility—"

"Ehhhhyiiiiiiiii!" Donnie shrieked as he blasted
out of the Commvee holding Cordelia's teacup in
the air.

Cordelia and the Colonel dashed out after him.

"Return that teacup at once!" Cordelia bellowed.
"Radcliffe, do something!"

"Not as fast as I used to be, Cordy," the Colonel
replied.

Jabbering incoherently, the untamed boy
streaked between Nigel and the camera.

"Donnie!" Marianne scolded.

But Donnie's eyes lit up as he spotted a half
dozen baboons who seemed captivated by his every
move. They quickly surrounded him, trying to
snatch the teacup from his hands as if it were a
prize.

Nigel looked on in fascination and continued his
narration.

"Ah, a troop of baboons, playful primates of the
Serengeti—"

"Nigel!" Cordelia shouted. "That china has been
in the family since Queen Victoria reigned!"

Nigel dived after Donnie, but missed him completely and tumbled into the watering hole.

A baboon began chasing Cordelia.

"Shoo! Shoo, you beastly thing!" she shrieked.

As the Colonel tried to nab Donnie with his umbrella he hooked him by the waistband of his shorts, and gave him a wedgie. Delighted, Donnie began his wedgie dance.

And the fascinated baboons imitated the wild boy, step for step.

As Eliza, Debbie, and Darwin approached the chaos Eliza said to her sister, "Deb, you know you can't ever tell anyone I talk to animals, right?"

Debbie rolled her eyes and gestured toward the grasslands beyond. "We live in Nowhereville. Who am I gonna tell?" She strode toward her parents.

"Debbie, I'm serious!" Eliza was suddenly worried. Now that the danger from the poachers was over, what if Debbie decided to blab to their parents about her secret gift?

She ran to catch up with Debbie. "When I got my powers back, I had to agree to a condition. I can't ever tell."

Debbie stopped and turned on Eliza, suddenly suspicious. "Uh-huh . . ."

"And if *you* ever tell . . ."

Debbie glared at her, waiting.

Eliza gulped. "You'll turn into a baboon."

Debbie blinked a moment. She glanced at the

watering hole, where Donnie was dancing with a wild fan club of hairy, purple-bottomed . . . baboons?!

"A *BABOON?!*" Debbie shrieked. "But—but then I'd have to live my life with a BIG . . . PURPLE . . ."

Before she could sputter the dreaded word, a conga line of baboons danced by, imitating Donnie's wedgie dance.

Cordelia watched in dismay, but Nigel and Marianne joined in the dance. When the Colonel gallantly held out his arm, Cordelia at last gave in and began to dance with the rest of them.

Donnie grabbed Darwin and dragged him into the fun too.

As a few baboons danced right past Debbie she glared at her sister. "Eliza! This is *so* unfair!"

"What is, Debbie?" Marianne asked over the noise as she boogied by.

Eliza and Debbie looked at each other, then quickly said at once: "Nothing, Mom."

Debbie stalked over to the Commvee to sulk. But Eliza stayed and watched the scene.

England had been okay for a little while, but Eliza was like her father. She was happiest back in the wild.

She looked around as the sun set on one of her favorite places in the world.

They would stay here for a while. Then they'd

load up the Commvee and move on to another new place. Another camp, another story, another adventure.

And it didn't really matter where they went. As long as she was with her family, traveling the world, Eliza knew she was home.

African elephant: There are two types of elephants in the world: Asian and African. The African elephants have larger ears, and both the male and female have tusks. The tusks are made of dentine, like human teeth, and are used to dig for water, carry things, tear bark off trees, and fight. An elephant can live up to seventy years and has no real predator—except for people, who hunt them for their tusks. The ivory tusks have been used to make jewelry, artwork, carvings—even piano keys! (Piano makers now use plastic.) In 1970 there were 1.3 million elephants in Africa. Now only 600,000 are left in the wild; 5,000 are forest elephants. The ivory trade became illegal in 1990, but the demand for ivory products continues, and illegal poaching is still a major threat to the survival of these intelligent animals.

Black rhino: The black rhino isn't really black—it just looks black because of the dark-colored soil it likes to wallow in! Rhinos have been on Earth for fifty thousand years, but now they are almost extinct. Poachers have hunted rhinos because they could sell their horns for medicinal or ornamental uses. Between 1970 and

1992, the number of black rhinos dropped from 65,000 to 2,300. But thanks to conservation groups working to protect them, their numbers are increasing.

Cheetah: Cheetahs are the fastest animals on land. They can run up to sixty miles an hour—but only for a short distance. They crouch in the tall grasses of the plains, then spring after their prey. Poachers have hunted them for their valuable coats. People have cleared thousands of acres of their habitats for farmland. Now scientists estimate that there are fewer than fifteen thousand left in the wild.

Serengeti: Tanzania's famous Serengeti National Park is a sprawling six thousand square miles of open grassy plains. A visit here is like a trip back in time—before hunters and poachers destroyed much of East Africa's wildlife. Millions of animals, including cheetahs, zebras, gazelles, elephants, lions, rhinos, chimpanzees, and giraffes roam the Serengeti plains.

Tanzania: The largest country in East Africa, Tanzania is a land of vast plains, lakes, and mountains. It's home to Africa's highest peak—Mount Kilimanjaro, a snow-capped mountain that's made up of three extinct volcanoes. The people speak Swahili and English.

About the Author

Cathy East Dubowski has written more than one hundred books for children, including The Wild Thornberrys *Gift of Gab* and *Hanging On to Home* (cowritten with husband Mark Dubowski). She lives in Chapel Hill, North Carolina, with Mark and their two daughters, Lauren and Megan. And while they don't have Eliza Thornberry's special talent, they do their best to talk to their pets Macdougal and Morgan (golden retrievers), Carster and Coconut (hamsters), Ramona (guinea pig), and Coco-Puffs (rabbit). Cathy writes on a computer in her office in an old red barn, which she shares with various insects, lizards, and the occasional field mouse.